SOULS PASS

Charlene Penfold

EROTIC ROMANCE

SIREN

Siren Publishing, Inc.
www.SirenPublishing.com

A SIREN PUBLISHING BOOK
IMPRINT: Erotic Romance

SOULS PASS

ISBN: 978-1-62241-175-7

First Printing: July 2012

Cover design by Jinger Heaston

Printed in the U.S.A.

PUBLISHER
Siren Publishing, Inc.
www.SirenPublishing.com

DEDICATION

I would like to dedicate my first book being published in the memory of my Poppa, who passed away this January 2012, and to Momma, who was the first person to read this book and give me the courage to continue when the cards were down.

I would also like to dedicate it to the rest of my family for their continued support through the years. Their advice and criticism has been well worth the wait.

A note to my readers—be patient and persistent. Dreams can come true.

Aunt Brenda
Thanks for all
the encouraging words
Love Charlie

SOULS PASS

CHARLENE PENFOLD

Chapter One

All one could see and hear for a mile down the road was the lights and sirens, a police car leading an ambulance down the road. If JFK hadn't already been shot, one would have thought he had been now, with the number of squad cars speeding down the road. They were going to the Gordon Estate that lay on the other side of the bridge. Mr. Ivan Gordon was a very powerful, respected man in this small community of Soul's Valley.

Friends knew that he had been ill for some time, so there was no surprise to the neighbors to see the ambulance.

Sandra was sobbing uncontrollably. He didn't know what else to do to help his wife through this difficult time. All he could do was hold her until she stopped. It had only been months since the loss of her mother. Everyone at the Mystical Thoroughbred Breeding Ranch was in mourning. Philip had no idea how to get in touch with his wife's sister. He knew in his heart that that was what she really needed.

In between sobs, she managed, "Phil, I need to find Amy. I know that she has a place in New York. I don't know if she keeps in touch with Hank or not. Please, she should hear this from me, not someone else."

"Honey, I will do everything that I can, I will get her here," Philip said to his sobbing wife.

Amy was in Hollywood doing a photo shoot for a new and up-and-coming jewelry designer. She had never modeled jewelry before. This was fun and different. She was having a blast. Although the show was considered to be a "classic," the original *Teens of Beverly Hills* was one of her favourites. She loved the cast, and now she was modeling Tori Mahaffey's newest creations. It had been a two-day event, and on the last day, Tori invited her out to lunch. She was an amazing person, fun loving, creative, and so very busy these days. She had lots on her plate with the debut of her new jewelry line and the guest appearance on the new *Teens of Beverly Hills*. She had her up-and-coming book launch and her son, Liam's, birthday party, and she also wanted to be with Sean, which meant traveling.

Now those two were hot in love with each other. That was as plain to see as the nose on ones face. Besides Amy's own parents' love affair with each other, she had only seen that same kind of passion for each other in Tori and Sean that she only wished that she could find, but for right now she would settle on her career. It made her happy.

They were sitting in the studio office reviewing the final pictures for Tori to choose for her ad campaign. "Amy, you enhance the beauty of these pieces. I'm not surprised. I have to admit that I had some reservations in asking you to model them. I didn't want the competition. But there's not, you only enhance their beauty. Thank you," she said, getting up from her seat to give her a hug and lay out the ones that she wanted to use.

Amy was in the air on her way back home when her BlackBerry rang. She dug into her handbag and pulled it out to answer it. "Hello, Sophie, what's up? I'm on my way back to New York, should be there in about six hours."

"That's good, we need to talk about your next assignment, already lined up for you when you get back. I talked with Tori herself, and she is so pleased with the pictures and job that you did for her. Good job, darling. Hold on a minute, the office line is ringing…Hello, yes this is she…I have her on my other line. Yes, I will tell her to call." She only heard part of the call before her cell died.

She was listening to the morning news on the plane, not really paying any attention until they announced that Mr. Ivan Gordon had just died of a massive heart attack at his Soul's Valley mansion best known as Mystical Ranch. Tears started to well up in her eyes. She knew that he was not well but still could not bring herself to go home, to face her failures, to see the disappointment in Daddy's eyes. That would be too much.

She was not surprised her family hadn't called. They had not been very close for years. It was for this reason that she didn't reside on the estate anymore. The mistake was letting her ex-husband, Hank, get between them. Hank was the type of man that didn't want Ivan's help in anything. All Hank wanted to do was prove that he could be a better horse breeder than the Gordons. He had started out as a hired hand at the Gordons' Estate when he was just fifteen years old and worked his way up to the position of ranch manager, with Ivan's teaching and guidance along the way.

Something happened one day after Amy turned eighteen. He noticed that she had become a very strong-willed woman. Unlike her twin sister Sandra, who was just minutes older. Sandra was every inch as beautiful as Amy, but she used her looks and not her brains like Amy did to get what she wanted.

Sandra had had her eye on Hank Meadows from the first day she had seen him at the ranch. He was what she wanted, but to her dismay, he never seemed to notice her, not the way he always noticed Amy. And that is what started the family feud.

With her insecurities in the beauty department, she felt like a goddess when Hank would flirt with her and take her out on dates. Daddy told her to stay away from him, that he would just use her to make Sandra jealous, but Amy didn't want to believe that, nor did she want to believe all the rumors that Hank was "a real ladies' man who would love them and leave them."

When she had announced just after her twentieth birthday that she had accepted Hank's marriage proposal, her father had flipped. All he could think about was how this was going to infuriate Sandra, his princess. Daddy's first reaction was to keep them close, so he offered them land to build a ranch on their northern country retreat, just north of Bobcaygeon. Much to her surprise, Hank accepted.

Their wedding was not a huge celebration, just something small, elegant yet traditional. To love, honour, and leave out the obey, until death did they part, meant a lifetime to her, but apparently Hank found himself a sweet little tart to bed and get pregnant. She didn't have the heart to tell her family what had happened, though she imagined that they already knew. After all she was still a Gordon, despite her accidental break into the fashion world from modeling her closest friends' clothes at a fashion show in Toronto. A well-known clothes designer saw her and thought that she was a natural beauty, landing her into the world of fashion modeling, and now she was constantly in the limelight.

A year after her divorce, while she had been traveling the globe for *Vogue* magazine, she had gotten a telegram, dated March 10, announcing that her mother had passed away on February 13th, the day before her twenty-fifth birthday that was eight months ago. She had been keeping a close eye on her father and had been told about his triple heart bypass only a month after their mother's death.

Ivan Gordon had been a strong man, but seeing his family slowly fall apart was a nightmare for him to watch. He had to unite his family again. Ivan had sent a letter to her, which she kept on her person at all times. She pulled it out to read, to feel close to him again.

My Dearest Shadow:

I have missed seeing your lovely smile, the one that you have so inherited from your mother, as well as her grace and beauty and, yes, her "take-no-shit-from-anyone" attitude. I have made a terrible mistake by pushing you away when you wed Hank.

You must understand that I had been trying to protect your sister. She is now married. Surely you must have heard. He treats her well and she loves him, forgetting about your little childhood games that you both had played. I just hope that you have found that same happiness...

Although she has carried this letter with her for quite some time, this was the first that she had read it and became aware that her father had knowledge of her divorce and did not blame her or have a "told you, he was no good" attitude toward her, but he in fact loved her and was quite proud of her accomplishments. She held his letter in her hand, close to her heart, as she watched the news of his death.

Oh Daddy...how I have missed you. And now I will never be able to tell you the things that you needed to hear the most.

It was the longest flight that she had ever taken. She couldn't get off the plane fast enough. To hear of her father's death this way. She needed to be with her sister now. Damn, her cell was dead, so she used the airport pay phone to arrange for a driver to take her to Soul's Valley. She had some time while she waited and called Sophie back to let her know what she was doing and that the next assignment would have to wait, or get someone else...so many things had to be done. She nervously dialed Sophie and told her of the events only to learn that the phone call was from Amy's sister that she took while talking to her. She understood and would look after everything on this end. And she promised to call Susie, her housekeeper, and let her know.

Chapter Two

It was about an eight-hour drive from New York to Soul's Valley. Sitting in the backseat, the past wandered into her mind. She decided to let Hank keep their ranch, Huckleberry, on the condition that he buy it from her and give her first option to buy back should he decide to sell. It was her father's land that she didn't really want to let go of. She held the mortgage for him. As memories of her childhood came flooding back, she couldn't hold back the tears any more.

She sat back there staring out the window, quietly sobbing, as she rode to the estate up around the winding roads, with the beauty of the surrounding quarry rocks lining the way. It was the longest drive that she could remember. This whole day has been long, and she felt that the night was only going to get longer. As they drove up the long, narrow driveway and were approaching the house, she saw the reporters and their vans. She told the driver to use the delivery route to the stables then follow the drive up around to the house at the back door and that he could come in through the kitchen door. The stables held a secret entrance up to the house.

She and Sandra used it a lot when they were teens sneaking in after curfew. Daddy knew about it and thought it was funny. Momma would scold him for not disciplining them.

She entered the kitchen and looked around, almost forgetting how cozy the room was. It made her feel welcome all over again.

"You must be Amy. I've heard a lot about you and seen lots of your pictures!" He paused for a breath as he took in her beauty. "How did you make it past all the reporters?" asked this tall, muscular man.

This must be Sandra's husband, she thought to herself, not having seen any pictures of him.

Startled by his voice at first, in total awe, she was daydreaming about this incredibly handsome man. With biceps that told their own story, he was tall, well above average looking, certainly not her usual dating material, the whole cowboy look. What was she doing? She didn't know what to say. She felt her face tighten and knew the look that she had just given this man.

Shaking her head to clear her daze, she said, "Sorry…yes, I'm Amy, and you must be…" She left a spot for him to jump in.

"I'm Rick Durham, the new ranch manager. I'm so sorry about the loss of your father. He was a great man and well respected in this community. He will be missed. It must be devastating for you!"

"Yes." She felt like she could talk to this man for forever and tell her deepest secrets and desires to him. "I never had the chance to say good-bye!" A few tears slipped down her cheek. He stepped closer and followed through with his urge to wipe away her tears. They both felt the electricity between them. "Surely then you must know about the passage underground from the stables to the house?" she replied.

"No, but I do now. Can I help you in with your bags?" He looked around for them, just as Sandra came into the kitchen screeching.

"Amy!" Sandra was ecstatic as she kept walking toward her with open arms. "I'm so glad that you came…I've missed you so!" Tears were spilling down her cheeks. Her sister was here. Things would get better now.

"Sandi…I've missed you all so much, too! Sorry to hear about Momma, I wished that I could have been here for you all when she passed away…but I didn't get word 'til weeks after! But I am here now!"

The two girls walked arm in arm into the family room, where the drapes had been pulled to give them privacy from the reporters and cameras. Her thoughts were still back in the kitchen, thinking about their new ranch manager, Rick Durham. There was a tall, muscular, blondish-haired man standing at the fireplace with his arm over the winged-back chair, which sat a small, young boy. She could see the resemblance to his father, the man standing behind.

As if she could read Amy's mind, Sandra introduced the people in the room. She noticed Amy looking around into some of the unfamiliar faces.

"Amy…this is my husband, Philip Larson, and our son Andrew. You remember Patti, Joe, and Anna, the house staff. Now some of these faces may not be so familiar…there's Bob, our horse trainer, Felix, the assistant manager, and of course you had the pleasure of meeting Rick in the kitchen." She certainly did enjoy the pleasure of meeting him. He was one handsome fella. Although she looked around the room into the unfamiliar faces, she was drawn back to one in particular, Rick's.

"Nice to meet and see you all. Thank you for being here. It means a lot to us," she said, looking around the room. Tears were beginning to well up in her eyes, she continued to be strong and fought them back. She could not let go now.

"If no one objects, I think I will just go upstairs and lie down for a bit. It's been a long day. Again thank you." She excused herself from the room and wandered her way upstairs, having forgotten how the bottom and top stair creaked.

Once upstairs, she found herself in their parents' room, and she could still smell that mixture of Old Spice and Morning Dew, their two fragrances mixed together. She lay across what once used to seem like a huge bed, just remembering the image of their parents and the funny little things that they did. She could remember the way Daddy would smell Momma's hair after zipping up her dress or doing up her necklaces and Momma's laughter, as she said it tickled when his beard would rub against her neck when he did…*Oh, how I miss those days.* A tear rolled down her cheek. She held their wedding picture that sat on Daddy's bureau.

"There you are…you all right?" Sandra opened the door and walked toward her. "You don't have to explain to me about Hank! I know what he did. I'm so sorry, Amy," Sandra said as she, too, lay across the bed. They both just lay there for a few minutes looking into each others' eyes. So much time had passed, yet it felt like they were teens again.

"I'm so happy for you, Sandi…That you found someone! Daddy wrote to me just before…but his letter never said anything about a child," she finally broke out.

"Philip's first wife died giving birth to Andrew, and I love them both so much! Daddy introduced us. Philip had just taken over the marketing firm that Daddy dealt with for the horses and asked him over for supper to meet the team. Momma fell in love with him instantly. We started dating and, like a real gentleman, he courted me with flowers and candy. Oh, Amy, you will love him, too! Just wait and see."

"I'm sure that I will!" She paused and spoke before she really thought about it. "I think I might sell my penthouse and move back here, if that's all right with you?" she asked with a concerned look on her face, one that said that she was not certain that her sister would want her living under the same roof again.

"Amy, Amy…Don't have to ask. This is your home as much as it is mine! You know…we're your biggest fans! We have all your covers and all the pictures from other magazines and newspaper articles. I'm sorry about Hank! But you seemed to bounce right back!" She got up from the bed, walked to the closet, and reached down for the scrapbook that their parents kept and brought it back over to the bed. She opened it to show her sister just how proud they all were of her…tears had found their way back as they flipped through the pages.

Several moments had passed before she found her voice again. "Sandi…that's only because I threw myself into my work. I didn't refuse any assignments, and then they offered me the cover page for

Vogue—I could not refuse, the trip around the world to see all the exotic places, all expenses paid, the best hotels."

"Did you meet any new and exciting men? Do tell, sis, and don't leave out any of that juicy stuff."

"I met a few interesting men, none that I wanted to make it serious with. They just didn't steal my heart. I want what Daddy and Momma had. I want him to look at me the way that Philip looks at you." Sorrow filled her heart as she spoke to her best friend.

It was almost like the old days and the girls continued to talk, trying to catch up with each other's lives.

They had never seen so many people show up to a funeral before. Ivan Gordon was a very powerful, respected man. People they never met before came up to them and gave their condolences and wished them well for the future. The sermon was beautiful, Reverend Green did such a wonderful job, and Momma's sister said a few words about Daddy and the things that he did in his earlier years. It made people laugh with ease. After the services, they all drove over to the estate, to the family burial plot, where a few more words were said by close friends.

After everyone left the cemetery to go back to the house for refreshments, it gave her a chance to say good-bye to both of her parents.

She had been trying to avoid Rick Durham all day. He was just too damn hot. His body-builder abs, the pecs and biceps, were all visible from the way that his shirt fit. Oh, and that tight tush. It was hard to avoid looking at it in those cowboy dress jeans. Just watching him she could still feel the electricity from his touch the night before. Ah, saved by the bell…

"Hank…" She walked right past Rick to see Hank Meadows, the ex-husband. She had no idea why he was here. She hugged him and whispered in his ear, "What the hell are you doing here?" smiling all the while so people wouldn't notice.

"Well…I have the utmost respect for your father, you know," he retorted.

"All right, but please do not cause a scene. Thank you for coming. It actually means a lot," she said as she stepped aside.

"Who is the barbarian that keeps staring at us?" Hank asked.

Rick was watching Amy. She was a captivating, breathless beauty, and he had never seen such a wonder before. Yeah, he'd seen other pretty women, but nothing like her. She just had this aura about her, and he could still feel her soft skin when he wiped away her tears the night before. She did look a lot like her sister. The similarities were plenty, almost identical, yet he was not attracted to Sandra. Her sexy curves, long, wavy auburn locks. He could not help himself from staring at her. Of all places to get a hard-on, he thought to himself, turning away.

She looked around, but the only man that would fit that description was Rick Durham. She looked at Hank, who still wore that jealous look in his eyes. The look that started their marital problems, as far as she was concerned.

"That's the ranch manager! I have not had a chance to chat with him yet! On another note, your payment to the bank was late! Why?" she asked, still looking in the direction of Rick. He was mesmerizing. She was not quite sure why, yet, that she was so drawn to him. She was not in a place in her life right now to take on a new lover. Wow, back that train of thought up…she was thinking of Rick in terms of a lover? What was she thinking? She didn't know the first thing about this man, and already she was having these bizarre fantasies of Rick in bed doing wonderful things to her.

"Amy…Amy…are you listening to me?" He gave her a gentle poke to finally get her attention, stopping her in her tracks. "Don't start. This is not the place or the time to get into an argument. It was made, and that's all that should matter!" he replied rather sharply and sounded a little annoyed that he had to get her attention away from that "barbarian."

Chapter Three

It was about seven that night when the house started to feel empty. Everyone had left. Amy didn't normally drink, but somehow her glass seemed to have a bottomless supply of scotch in it, and it was starting to take its effect on her. She had been sitting in the study looking through some old family albums. They were reminiscing of days gone by and what their precious daddy was like growing up. Amy remembered one time going into town with Daddy to the feed mill. They had screwed up the order horribly. Man, was he furious. She had never seen that side of her father. He tore a strip off one side and down the other of that poor manager. But the feed mill never screwed up the order again.

She decided to go for a walk down to the stables to clear her head that was starting to ache. She walked into the stables, and there he was. Rick was leaning up against Fate's stall. He was chitchatting with the horse. *He is something else, hot and sexy at the same time.* Although she had been avoiding him for this reason, she had the need for distraction.

"Hi there," she said as she came up to him to stand beside him.

"Hi there yourself. How are you feeling? I am truly sorry about your dad. He was an awesome guy to work for and with. I really respect what he has been trying to do with Mystical," he replied in a soft tone as he bumped her side in a friendly manner.

"Thanks, I really appreciate hearing that. I hope that you plan on staying around. I mean, now that Daddy is gone, we will need your guidance and help even more. And from what Sandra has told me,

Daddy really respected you and your opinions as well. So tell me, Rick, what brings you to all the way to Soul's Valley?"

"I was looking for a change of place. Guess you could say that I was getting restless in my old job back home." He was taking in her beauty.

"Really. And where is 'back home'?" she asked, turning her attention back to Fate.

"Alberta is home. But most of my family is scattered around the globe these days. What's it like being in the limelight constantly?"

"It gets tiring some days. I don't always enjoy everyone knowing my business. I think it's time that I head back up to the house. Thanks for the conversation."

She turned, not looking where she was putting her feet, and *wham,* she tripped over something and hit her head a good one on a can. Rick immediately went to her side. He looked around and saw the rope that someone carelessly left lying around that she must have tripped over. Also seeing the can and the little bit of blood, he was now concerned that she may have a concussion. He lightly slapped her on the face a couple of times to wake her. She was barely audible mumbling about something. He was only thinking about saving her the embarrassment of her condition as he carried her back to his bunk.

He kept her awake as long as he could, only letting her fall asleep when he felt comfortable enough that she was in no immediate danger. When she woke the next morning, her surroundings were unfamiliar. She couldn't be dreaming, could she? He was leaning over her, smelling like…Old Spice? Daddy? *No no no no*, she shook her head…Looking down under the covers, she saw that she was still fully clothed.

"I think that you will be fine. That's a nasty little bump on your head, though." The voice was familiar, but still her eyes were not quite focused on anything yet. She still had this image of Rick in her head. He was shirtless, lying next to her, rubbing her shoulders and back. Oh, how strong those hands were, her head resting on his chest and her hands occasionally rubbing his abs…oh, those abs, nice and strong, feeling his little soft kisses on her forehead and on her lips. She was still thinking what it would be like to have wild, passionate love with this man…"Where am I?" she sat up asking.

"You are in my bunkhouse, Amy." He sensed that she was still a little confused and embarrassed judging by the colour added to her cheeks. He was not sure if she remembered sleeping in his arms last night. The things that he would have loved to do to her last night. He kissed her, and it was oh so sweet. She kissed him back with a passion that he still felt in the bottom of his gut and not-so-pure thoughts, but he could not take advantage of her in her state.

"Thanks." With a few more stumbles, she got up and left for the house, thinking along the way, how embarrassing. She remembered lying there in his bed, kissing him. Oh, those sweet kisses that tasted like Swiss mocha. Those strong hands, arms…oh, that tush and the bulge in his jeans. Could he be that well endowed? *They do say it's not how large a man is, but rather how he can use it…*giving a little laughter as she walked, not believing that she was having these thoughts again, she remembered everything that didn't happen last night and everything that did, and she would have let him take their kisses to the next level if he led them there, but he seemed to back off.

Over the course of the next couple of days, she ran into Rick several times while visiting Fate, her beloved horse. She tried a few times to strike up conversation but found that she was still somewhat embarrassed from the other night. One day while Amy was combing out Fate's mane, Felix stopped by for a little chat. She asked some questions about Rick, to learn what he was like as a manager and how the others liked having him as a boss. She learned that Rick didn't ask the guys to do anything that he himself would not do. If that meant shoveling shit from the stalls, then so be it. She also learned that he was well liked by the others and that he could be fun to be around but also had a serious side. Overall, the guys really respected him.

She couldn't get out of Soul's Valley fast enough, in order to put as much distance between her and Rick. Sophie came to the funeral, they chatted for a little bit, and she told her that she had an assignment lined up in Milan if she wanted it, but it started in five days. Amy told Sophie that she would think about it. She jumped on it. She loved being in Italy. She had a fabulous time the last time she visited. It would give her the distance that was needed. There was too much temptation with Rick. She had been trying to convince herself that her career was all that she needed, that she would never find the kind of love that her parents shared. The kind of love that she thought that she had with Hank, but he destroyed it. And she was having a hard time believing that any man could be trusted again.

It was a couple of days after the funeral, and they were sitting in the family room enjoying peace and quiet. Andrew had been in bed for a couple of hours when Amy boldly announced, "I have another assignment. It's taking me to Milan. I will be leaving in the morning."

"Amy…" There was sorrow in her sister's voice as she spoke softly. "I'm not ready for you to leave. We have so much catching up to do." She looked at her and didn't understand the sudden change. "Amy, just the other day you said that you were selling your condo to move back here."

Looking at her sister, she felt the grief and saw the quizzical look. "Sandi, this is what I do. I'm still selling the condo. I can't stop now. I need to get away." Tears were welling up. She got up from the comfy sofa and walked over to her sister to give her a hug. "It's going to be okay, I will be back, it's only for a week, ten days to be exact."

Patting her beloved sister on the back, Sandra couldn't help but wonder if it had anything to do with Hank showing up at the funeral, or perhaps Rick. She had noticed that her sister had not come back to the main house the night of the funeral and saw the look of passion on her face when they met up in the kitchen the next morning.

Philip stepped up to embrace the two girls. "Ames, it's just bad timing."

"I know, Phil, but it can't be helped."

Later that night, while down in the stables visiting with Fate, Rick entered the stables. She knew that he was there before he even spoke.

Walking up to her, "Hi there. How are things going? Did you know that he prefers this brush over the one that you have?" he said as he handed her the new silver brush.

"Hi there yourself. I did not know that. How do you know what he prefers? Things are going, it is a little tough at times, but we are strong like Daddy and we will make it through this. Thanks for asking," she replied, taking the brush that he offered without really missing a stroke.

"I brush him every day. And for some reason the silver one seems to keep him the calmest," he said with a hint of laughter in his voice.

"Oh, really. I never seemed to notice before. I guess you are right. I'm leaving in the morning for Italy." The last part she just seemed to blurt out, as if she thought that he really cared what she was doing.

"What's it like, traveling the world? Do you ever get lonely for your family, I mean?" he asked as he stood beside her. His lower arm brushed upside her shoulder. He could feel that same electricity as the first time he touched her tearstained face only nights ago. He wondered why she told him that she was leaving.

"Yes, I get lonely for my family, but this is the type of work that I choose to do, and I like going to different places, meeting different people, trying new things. Don't you?" She turned the table back to him. She noticed that he became quiet, as if he was lost in thought.

It took what seemed like long, dragged-out minutes for him to respond. "I used to travel a fair amount. But like you, this is what I choose to do for work. I believe that I will travel more with the races that we are going to enter and win." He left it at that as he turned and left her standing there with that thought.

The next morning was a tearful good-bye, and she reassured Sandra that she would be back really soon. Before she knew the time would have flown by.

She was greeted at the airport by Sophie, who gave her all the details that she would need once she arrived in Milan, such as her hotel reservation, the name of her driver, et cetera, and that a package would be waiting for her at the hotel. Best of all, she wished her luck and to have fun.

She checked her baggage and boarded the plane. The last couple of days had been such a blur. She felt that she had been on the go constantly. Thoughts of Rick kept invading her mind. She could not get that fabulous smile, the kisses that they shared, or his caring eyes out of her mind. The eleven-hour flight was much needed and it was time for sleep. She never had any issues sleeping while flying. Her dreams were pleasurable, almost lifelike. She was having amazing sex with Rick in the most unexpected places. But she woke in time, feeling somewhat refreshed.

Waiting in the lobby at the airport, she had a description of the guy that was to pick her up. *Ah, over there, he's holding up a sign.* "Grato, signora Gordon." Time to brush up on her Italian. She walked over in his direction.

"Sono signora Gordon." I am Ms. Gordon, she stumbled. He indicated to follow him to the car. He went and retrieved her luggage, brought it back to the waiting car, drove her to the Piazza Duca d'Aosta in Milan, helped her out of the car, and carried her luggage inside to the check-in desk.

"Ciao, sono signora Gordon. Vorrei controllare nella mia stanza, per favore e grazie," she said as she placed her passport on the front desk.

"Ciao, signora Gordon. Your Italian is a little rusty, but very well. Grato, we have your room ready for you, please sign our registry." The young lady spoke fluent English and handed her the package that Sophie had mentioned. The clerk motioned for the porter to help take her things to her room.

She decided to take a nice hot bubble bath to relax and help sleep. Jet lag was not just a word for her. Even though she slept for most of the eleven hours on the flight, she still felt somewhat tired. It was the events of the past several days that had her in a tailspin. First the six-hour flight from Los Angles to New York, the eight-hour drive to Soul's Valley, her father's funeral, Rick…Oh, yes, then there was Rick. Even halfway around the world he took residence in her heart. This was strange for her. Never before had a guy had her in such a fluster. *What am I going to do? I have fallen over this guy, and we haven't even had sex yet. Listen to me, yet, as if it will happen, what a fool. Relax, do the assignment, do some sightseeing, things that you couldn't do the last time you were here. Take some time for you.* All these thoughts were going through her mind.

As the tub filled, she read over the instructions for the first photo session scheduled for tomorrow, late morning, at the Castello Fountain found in front of the Szforesco Castle. A water feature was scheduled to start, then a few more shots around the outside of the castle itself. This should be fun. Work always helped to relax her. When the water was ready she climbed into the soaker tub. She lay there enjoying the bubble bath. Her insides felt the wave of sensual desire overcome her as she thought of the first time that she saw Rick. She woke up looking like a prune, and to cold water, climbing out and toweling off, she thought that she better call and request a wake-up call.

"Salve, questa è la signora Gordon in camera 1245. Vorrei chiedere a wake-up call for 8:00 a.m. Grazie." She hung up the phone and crawled into the big, fluffy bed. She didn't hear another thing until her phone rang, and she turned to look at the clock. It was her wake-up call. She reached for the phone to answer. "Ciao, servizio in camera, per favore e grazie."

"Room service, how can I help you?" Thank goodness, someone that spoke English. "Can I please have some café, with bacon and eggs—scrambled. Grazie." Hanging up the phone, she rolled out of bed and jumped into the shower.

Breakfast arrived, and she ate and finished getting ready to head downstairs to where Robert was waiting to take her to the photo shoot. It went really well and they took about five shots a piece at about ten different angles, some standing in the fountain and then some standing around it, tourist-like shots. The assistants were really nice and spoke near-perfect English. They had lunch brought in and she only wanted a salad as she wasn't hungry after her big breakfast. They shot a few more pictures.

Joey, the photographer, directed her in how he wanted the poses. At the castle they had her change into a hot dress that was this sexy little number. It was a *V* cut all the way down to her belly. *If Rick could see me in this...* There she went again...*Stop it, Amy, focus.* About an hour later, Joey said he was pleased with the shots that he got and called it a wrap for the day, and he would see her tomorrow.

The weather was an unusual high for October. She changed back into her walking shorts and wandered around the castle for a little longer, viewed the art at the Civiche Raccolte d'Arte Antica Applicata museum, then had Robert take her back to the hotel. Once back at the hotel, she decided to take a walk along the Via Dante. As she walked along Via Dante, thoughts filled her mind of Rick and how she would like to have him here with her, to show him these beautiful sights. She wasn't sure if this was something that he would enjoy or not, but it would be interesting to find out, to learn more about him, to have him in her arms, feel his warmth and love, as in the night that she spent in his bed. *Jeepers, thousands of miles from home, and I still can't get him out of my head. This is not working.*

She thought to herself, do this assignment and go home, confront these feelings you are having for Rick, see if he has the same feelings. She continued along and did some shopping. Just after dinner, she decided to call her friends Gina and Kelly and see if they wanted to go out clubbing. She had to have something to do with all this pent-up energy to keep her mind off of Rick. Since it was the fashion centre of the world, Milan never seemed to sleep. They went to several clubs and listened to some music. A guy tried to pick her up, but she politely declined the free drink and dance. The waiter came over. "Posso avere qualcosa da bere?"

"Amerei uno Scotch e acqua—Scotch and water. Ringraziarla," she replied. She and the girls were having a blast. They were reminiscing over their past outings and ex-boyfriends and they were helping to keep her mind off Rick. They danced some and drank plenty more booze. About 2:00 a.m. she had to call it quits. She left the girls, who wanted to party some more, but she had an early call tomorrow. They all agreed to meet up for dinner before going to the theatre. She was happy that she called them.

That afternoon she had arranged to get tickets to the Teatro alla Scala, the famous Italian theatre, to see the Ballets Russes, and she just had to see it while she was here.

She had been having a blast this time around in Milan, working hard for Joey and the photo shoot, clubbing with the girls over the last eight days. It was her last night in Milan. Dinner with the girls and then the Teatro was on the agenda for tonight. The final shots were done inside the castle and around the different art pieces. Joey was really pleased with the outcome and the time frame. They only worked about three hours today, so he called it a wrap. Joey gave her a hug and kiss on the cheek and wished her well and said that he looked forward to the next assignment they would share. She decided to go do some more shopping. She had noticed the type of handbag that Sandra carried at home, remembered passing this boutique yesterday on her walking excursion, so she asked Robert to take her there. Walking in and looking around, this place was fabulous. The clerk asked if he could help. "Posso esserle d'aiuto?"

"Si, amerei questa borsetta—yes, I would like this handbag." She pointed to the Italian-leather backpack style. "Quanto lo fa è costato—how much does it cost?"

As the clerk retrieved the bag, he said, "Four hundred thirty euros, signora—I must also add that your Italian is very good." He let out a little chuckle with a smile.

"Si, grazie, I will take it." She looked at the basket of beautiful silk scarves. "This, too, oh, and can you gift wrap the bag? Please and thank you."

"No problem, signora, be just a few minutes." The clerk left her and a few minutes later returned with her parcel.

She popped into another store, this one was shoes and boots, her fetish, and she bought three pairs of shoes and a new pair of boots.

She packed up everything before dinner, as she had a late flight out and didn't want to be packing up after the show tonight. The hotel was kind enough to hold it downstairs for her.

Dinner was fabulous. The girls talked about their next assignment and about Kelly's latest beau, Prince Charming, as Gina called him, saying that he was just too good to be true. They laughed and drank plenty of wine over dinner.

The theatre was awesome. She enjoyed the Ballet. She hadn't done that in a couple of years, either. If Rick had been here, it would have been an awesome place to work. What was that, a whole ten minutes that she hadn't thought of him? The assignment to Milan was a good decision—it was an enjoyable work environment.

Customs at the airport was no surprise. She declared the few items that she bought besides her shoes. She declared more than she spent, and declaring cost her a little extra expense. The guys laughed at her. "Voi e i vostri modelli scarpe—You models and your shoes." She laughed with them. She boarded the plane. Sleep was the plan. She watched the movie onboard and fell asleep for the remainder of the flight.

Chapter Four

Back home on the Mystical Ranch, Rick was trying to prepare their best stallion Autumn Fate, to breed with their broodmare, Mystical Mystery. One of Mysticals' best champions. Bob, who was also their breeding assistant, was not helping the situation. The horses just didn't want to cooperate with him today. Was it really that, or was it Amy? She had been on his mind constantly since she abruptly left. He thought that they might have something, but she didn't stick around long enough for him to find out. He tried to talk to Sandra about it, but she was still upset over Ivan's death and her sister's abrupt departure.

Damn you, Amy, I can't concentrate on the things that I need to. The guys are sensing that there is something wrong. I'm snapping at them for everything. I'm acting like a love-struck schoolboy.

He had to get out of here for a few days. He wanted to go to Kentucky and look at a racing champion there, Sir Lancelot. The stallion showed promise for breeding, and he had convinced Sandra and Philip that Mystical could use another well-bred stallion. He would make the arrangements and leave in the morning, leaving Felix in charge and getting Mystery to the teaser. They needed to start the process now, in order to get her ready for the first of the year, if they wanted her to foal this time next year.

Rick went over the instructions with Felix again as to what a teaser was and how it worked for them, as Felix was in training, learning the ropes. Mystical ranch used a teaser stallion to determine the mare's receptiveness to the advances of a male horse with regards to breeding. The act involved bringing the mare and stallion into contact with each other, usually with a fence between them. This was done to give an idea to the breeder if the mare would be receptive to the stallions' advances. He went on to explain that they usually used ponies or something small that was well educated. This helped with regards to the ease of handling the horses.

Amy returned to New York when she said she would. Coming back to the ranch was the right thing to do. After the first day back, she learned that Rick had left for a few days to go and look at another stallion for the ranch. She felt some wave of disappointment. She apologized to Sandra for leaving so suddenly but explained again that this was the way her life was, jaunting here and there on short notice. This again was why it was a good idea to move back to the ranch, that it would give her a sense of home and still give Sandra and her family the privacy that they would need. Besides at any given time, she was usually just a phone call away. Sandra was in the family room doing a little bit of studying for her law exam when Amy came downstairs. She brought with her the new handbag that she had bought for her. "Here, I have a small gift for you." She handed the wrapped box to Sandi, who was sitting in the wing chair near the fireplace.

"What is this? You don't need to buy me gifts," Sandi asked as she carefully opened the box, and a look of surprise and awe swept over her face. "It is absolutely gorgeous. I love it!" She stood to give her baby sister a big hug to thank her again for the present.

"It's nothing. I saw it and thought of you and that ratty old backpack that you carry around." They both were laughing and enjoying the intimate embrace.

It seemed like time had just flown past after the funeral. She had decided to take some much deserved "me" time, for a couple of reasons. One, to gain control, some anyway, over her life. Two, Daddy's death took its toll on her, and three, to figure out this obsession she had with Rick. And if she didn't take the time off, the camera would make her look fifty years old, even with makeup!

Rick returned, but it felt like he was avoiding her like she was the plague. How was she going to resolve her feelings if he wouldn't even talk to her? The conclusion that she arrived at was that he was not interested, and she had to let it go.

He returned to find that Amy had come home from Milan. He wanted to talk to her, but he thought that if she was going to avoid him that that was for the best, he would have to forget about her and move on. Thinking more about it, he didn't really need to get involved with a high-profile model, and he still couldn't risk being noticed. It had been nearly twenty years since his family was placed into the witness protection program. New identities were given to the whole family. His father was the district attorney that put away Philadelphia's crime lord Sontiago. Rick was only eleven at the time when his life had changed forever. He just realized the consequences should he be recognized by the remaining members of the Sontiago family. From things that he read and shows he had watched, he learned that these type of people never let it go, that they are always looking for the ones that did their family wrong. For the first time, he wanted to share all this with someone—Amy. But knew that he couldn't do that just yet. He couldn't risk putting her in danger. He didn't even share this part of his life with his first wife.

Amy noticed that her sister was sleeping in more these days and that she looked a little feverous. Walking past their room, she heard the sounds of her vomiting. Now she was concerned. Knocking but not waiting for a reply, she walked in. "Sandi…Are you all right?" she called out.

"I am okay, just a little under the weather is all. Too much stress." She tried to sound upbeat but was startled as she took the towel beside her and wiped her face as she responded. Sandra did not want to draw any more attention to herself. Just a few days ago, she did go and see the doctor, and she confirmed her own diagnosis.

Satisfied with Sandra's response, she left the room to go outside for a little fresh air. Just wandering around outside in the crisp winter air, which still had no snow for Christmas, she found herself standing in Rick's office. She didn't remember knocking on his door or even inviting herself in, but there she was, staring at him sitting behind her father's desk.

He got up and walked around her to close the door.

"Good morning, Amy, want to have a seat?" He gestured to the chair in front of her to sit.

"What can I do for you? Is there something wrong?" He continued to stand there.

She just shook her head in awe, admiring this handsome man standing before her. *Oh, how I yearn for those arms to be wrapped around me…*She had issues focusing. She could hear him saying something to her, but it sounded like the teachers on Charlie Brown. She again shook her head to clear her erotic thoughts.

"Sorry, I was just remembering Daddy in this office. I should have knocked first…" She covered up her real thoughts and daydreaming.

Rick stepped closer to her, now invading her personal space, and he could feel her hot, heavy breath against his chin. She was above average height for a woman, but not quite as tall as he. He lowered his head and took her chin to raise her mouth to his mouth, all in one swoop. He had his aching lips pressed firmly against her hot ones, kissing her the way a woman should be kissed. On instinct she embraced his kiss and wrapped him in her arms. He felt her moans. She wanted him, too. She shivered in his arms. Then she pushed away…

"This is not right, I can't do this…" She turned to walk away, but he grabbed her arm to stop her. He was not letting her walk away this time, not without answers.

"Amy, don't leave yet. We should talk about this." His voice was soft and caring. She knew that she should stay but couldn't.

"No, I need to get back to the house. It just won't work, I am on the move constantly…" She left it at that and ran out of the office, almost knocking over Felix in the process.

"What the hell just happened in here, boss? Why is Mrs. Meadows so distraught?" He shot his boss and friend a glance as he looked back to see her running toward the house.

Judging from his question, his assistant must not have witnessed the kiss. "She is one troubled lady. She came in here, for what I really don't know, saw me sitting behind the desk, and then darted back out the door." He hoped that this answered his question and curiosity. It seemed to satisfy him, and they returned back to work. There was a new load of straw to empty into the stalls and horses to feed.

Everyone that remained at the Gordon Estate was trying desperately to get ready for Christmas. It was a little hard, but they were managing. It was the first big holiday since both their parents' passing. The house, including the grounds, had been dressed for the festivities. Little Andrew was getting excited about Saint Nick. He was only seven days away.

After Andrew's announcement of how long it was until Saint Nick arrived, presents came to mind, and Amy still had things to buy. She was trying her best to be in the Christmas spirit. It was hard, considering Rick still filled her thoughts most of the time. She decided to go back to New York for a few days and do some shopping. And since she decided to sell the condo, she hadn't really been back to do any packing.

Her thoughts were of Macy's and Saks to pick up the few things that she wanted for Sandra and Andrew. Many new toys and books for Andrew, and a beautiful new scarf and to-die-for boots for Sandi. Philip was a different story. She had noticed the torn, old briefcase that he was carrying around. Walking around Fifth Avenue, she noticed a "Grand Opening" sign for Pianki, fine leather products. She walked in and right away saw it, a Pineider. The salesman noticed her looking at it, and he said, " The finest handmade luxurious collections of exclusive and expensive Italian leather goods have defined the tastes of royalty, statesmen, celebrities, and wealthy individuals since 1774." It was the perfect gift for Philip. She had to have it, and it was worth it. After four hours of shopping, her feet were aching, and she had enough. She hailed a cab to take her back to her condo.

She was about to step into the elevator that led to her penthouse when a male's voice called out to her. She turned around and there stood Larry Krump, the owner of the building and one of her most endearing friends. He had sent her a personal note apologizing for not being there at her father's funeral, but he was in the middle of a big merger and the shooting of the new season to *The Lackey*.

"Larry…Merry Christmas!"

"Amy…I heard that you are trying to sell your suite…Is there anything wrong? Can I help?" His strong voice sounded so sincere.

"No. Larry, there's nothing wrong. It's just, well, you know about my father, and, well, my sister and her family are all that I have left and I just want to be closer to them. That's all. Thanks, you are a good friend, and please do say hello to Lonnie for me."

"I will, and I will see what I can find for a buyer and at the best price for you. We are having a little gathering for New Year's, would you and your family like to join us? I am sure that a few more people won't matter to Lonnie. Matter of fact, I know that she will be glad to see you again."

"I would love to come, and I will let you know about the others. Okay?"

"Sure, see you there, then. Bye. You have yourself a merry Christmas and happy New Year!"

"Lucky Lonnie," she whispered as she entered the elevator once again.

"Pardon me, ma am?" asked the porter without turning his head.

"Nothing…"

The porter helped her into her apartment with all the packages that she had. She had given Susie the week off, so the place was deathly quiet.

"That will be fine there, thank you," she said, pointing next to the sofa, indicating for him to put her packages there and handing him a twenty. "Merry Christmas and happy New Year," she said.

"Thank you…ma am, you, too!" he replied, looking at the bill as he left the apartment.

She flopped her tired body down onto the sofa, pulling at her boots to remove them, glancing over at the phone table, where there seemed to be a stack of letters and bills. She noticed the red light flashing on her answering machine. Pushing herself up and practically dragging herself over, she pressed the button to hear the messages play. The recorder announced, "You have three messages!"

Message one—"Amy, darling…it's Sophie, you know, your agent. Darling, there's floods of offers coming in for you! We have another good assignment! It's a surprise. Give me a dingle when you hear my voice, darling."

Message two—"Amy…are you there? Damn, I hate talking into these things and you know it, so if you are there, pick up! You have been avoiding me for months now. Susie isn't a very good liar. I love you. Call me…Jack," his sincere, masculine voice said. Jack was tall, dark, and handsome, and he didn't even know just how good-looking he was. He had the muscles from working out every day, and he ran at least three miles every morning. What was her problem? Just a few days ago she was dreaming of Rick and having fantasies of him. She dumped Jack because she didn't want a relationship right now.

Message three—"Amy…it's Jack. I'm downstairs. Your doorman said you just went up, so please let me come up and see you."

"Goddamn it," she said as she dialed ten for the concierge.

"Yes, Mrs. 'M'…" answered Markus.

"Please send up Mr. Hayes."

"Yes, ma'am." Hanging up, he called over to Mr. Hayes, "You may go up now!"

Collecting his parcel, he entered the elevator in a trance, remembering her sunfire auburn hair, hazel-green eyes, baby-soft skin, sensational curves that every healthy man would fantasize about, and her personal smell, which was so sweet. He could not stop thinking about her. *Be careful, arousal happens just thinking about her. Oh, what she does to this body.* He thought of her, wanting to kiss those kissable lips, part them with his tongue, and dance around in her sweet mouth, tasting her. *Now look what you have gone and done to yourself…Cold shower…An erection is not what I need when she sees me…Down, boy, down.*

Since she heard his voice, it brought back memories of Paris. Last fall, Jack was everything Hank wasn't. Jack was more than average build, not meaning heavy as in fat, but he worked out at the gym, he wasn't obsessed with his body, either. He had jet-black, gorgeous hair, and the sexiest green eyes that made one melt when one looked into them. But she had to break it off. It was too soon after her divorce, and she didn't want him on the rebound. She knew that it would never work that way. She had ended it the night before she left on her world tour. Jack had made his presence known on several occasions over the past year, trying to convince her that they were right for each other.

The doorbell startled her and, realizing that she had to get up to answer it, she sauntered over.

Opening the door for him, she stepped back and gestured to the sofa. "Jack, please come in, have a seat." He shook his head. He didn't want to sit just yet. Instead he leaned in to give her a welcoming-home peck on the cheek.

"Amy…" he said after a long pause, jumping in with both feet was his usual style. "I have to know why you ended it. And I don't want to hear it was because of your tour, either! It's more than that. What did I do wrong?" he questioned. She could see the hurt in his eyes.

Jack didn't like being the dumpee. He needed Amy in more ways than one. It didn't take much for him to fall for her from the moment that he first saw her. He knew that he had to have her in his bed. He had been following her career around the globe, he knew that her parents had recently passed away, and that more recently, she just returned from Milan, Italy. He was there and saw her many times from a distance, but the timing just didn't seem right to approach her.

"Jack…you know that it's my lifestyle…I've learned the hard way, this is no life for a relationship, at least for me. Eventually you would grow to hate me, and become jealous of the other men in my life. It would seem like I'm spending more time with them than with you." She had just repeated almost word for word what Hank said to her when she left.

"Amy…" He paused for a just a moment. "I love you. I have from that first moment when we met in the café in Paris. There's no need for me to become jealous of the others. If you were to give us a second chance, I would be the lucky one, knowing that you cared about me. Our schedules are very similar. If we are committed to each other, then this traveling around bit isn't going to hurt us!" He had to convince her to take him back. His plan wouldn't work otherwise.

Before she could say another word, he had stepped closer and taken her into his arms, held her tight as he planted his anxious lips against her hot ones, and with little force parted them with his tongue. She was stunned at first but did not resist his kiss. It was hot, sensational, making her wet with wanting more of him. It wasn't the right time. "Jack," she said as she pushed him away. She cared about Jack. Maybe if she moved forward with this relationship, she could put Rick out of her mind. The problem with that was that she felt the electricity with Rick, just his touch. She really didn't feel it with Jack. Jack was her usual dating type, not Rick. But they had to take this slow and easy, although her body was telling her that she wanted him as much as he was saying that he wanted her. She felt his growing erection pushed up against her throbbing center. "I just don't know." She finished her train of thought as she stepped back from him.

He held out his arms a moment longer. "What do you have to lose?" Wanting her was the worst yet the best thing that he ever felt for any woman that he had ever been with. His days and nights were filled with fantasies and longings of her. At the best of times he felt it difficult to concentrate on the business at hand. Writing his articles, it was becoming harder to concentrate. He would start writing on the subject then it would turn into thoughts of her, writing those erotic thoughts to paper.

"We've got to take this real slow and easy, if I decide to try again?"

"Amy…I promise you won't be disappointed or hurt again. You'll see!" There was a silent pause as they just stood there looking at each other as their heated desire rose.

This time it was Amy that walked into his arms, putting her arms around his neck and planting a big wet kiss on his lips. Jack didn't waste any time wrapping his arms around her waist to draw her tighter into his embrace. Their kiss was heated, sending hot waves of passion down her body, and her nipples started to tighten with the need to have him caress them, feeling again his growing erection pressed firmly against her center, letting her know that it was just not her wanting this.

He started placing little kisses down her neck, behind her ears, the sensitive spot that drove her wild that he found shortly after their first encounter. Her hands wandered, entwining her fingers through his thick black locks, pressing his head firmly against her chest as he magically undid her blouse, revealing her larger-than-a-handful-size breasts. He was running his tongue over and around her areola and teasing her taut nipples, then gently taking them with his hands, squeezing and suckling. The sensations were sending her over the top. She slid her hands down his back, over his tight ass, clasping his cheeks in her hands.

Chapter Five

"Jack…" she whispered into his ear. "We need to stop," her raspy, husky voice was saying as she continued to find her way to the front of his pants and undid the button and zipper, pushing his pants down first with her hand as far as they would reach then lifting her leg to help move them to the floor, freeing her hands once again to find his erection. She slid one hand ever so lightly over his shaft, sending intense sensual sensations down his body, and started to stroke him as he continued to send kisses and puppy-dog licks over her breasts. He let out little groans and moans, telling her not to stop what she was doing.

Just at that moment, Jack scooped her up into his arms, stepping out of his pants that lay on the floor, and carried her toward the bedroom. It wasn't that he did not hear her recommendation that they should stop, he did. It was their need and their desires that continued to show that kept him going forward. Once in the bedroom, he laid her down on the bed, looking into her sexy eyes, the eyes that said yes to him. He had to ask to make sure that they were both on the same page. "Are you sure? Do we continue?" he asked her. This had to be what she wanted, too, if it was going to work!

"Yes, Jack, I want you, like I never wanted for anything before. I need you inside me." She spoke in a soft, husky voice as she shimmied further up on the bed to welcome his body.

Jack followed on to fulfill his lover's orders. He finished undressing her and took off his shirt then lay down next to her after he rolled on a condom he found in his shirt pocket. They continued right where they left off, caressing, fondling the other's body, exploring, as if it had been their first time together. There was no doubt, just being this close to her gave him instant erection, she was wet and waiting for him. He rolled over on top of her. With his knees, he parted her legs, and he ran his hands down over her hot, wet mound ever so slowly, touching her clit, making her squirm under his spell and touch.

"Jack, I don't know how much more I can take," she moaned into his shoulder.

"Don't worry, my love, it won't be long now. You are so hot and wet. Feel what you do to me." At that moment, he slid into her as if they were one. Rhythmically slow and easy, he enjoyed the feeling of her tight pussy around his ever-pressing cock, knowing that she was not far from her orgasm now. Her breathing was fast and raspy, and she ran her fingers and nails down his spine, gripping his ass, screaming in soft, husky tones, "Harder, harder, I'm coming, ooooh, my God" as she bit down on her bottom lip…and then he let go, too. He had been waiting for her. They just lay there for several minutes before he turned and looked into her tired but loving eyes, saying, "I have a Christmas present for you! Would you like to open it now?"

"Why don't you wait and save it for Christmas day and come with me to Soul's Valley and spend the holidays with my family? Unless you have other plans already?" she said out of the blue. She was supposed to be taking things slow with Jack. Inviting him back to the ranch was going to complicate things further. That was where Rick was! What was she doing taking Jack there, and why was she thinking of Rick here, of all places and times. Wasn't she trying to avoid seeing him again, imagining the passion that they could share in their lovemaking! Jack spoke again, breaking into her thoughts.

"That's not so far away from my office in Toronto. I can visit my family there, too! Will you come and meet them?" he asked as he continued to hold her in his arms. The warmth of her sweet, angelic body nestled against his.

She didn't realize just how happy she had made him.

A little later after their heated storm of intimacies, he asked, "Can I offer to take you out for a bite to eat? I don't know about you, but after our amazing lovemaking, it has made me a little hungry…for food!"

"All right, you twisted my arm. Where shall we go? Keep in mind that I may, no let me correct that, I will need to shower first and change my clothes…So give me ample time," she replied as she climbed off of the bed. The sheets were rumpled from their wild, passionate sex. She was not ready to call it lovemaking. She wasn't sure if she was in love with Jack, and to her, one needed to be in love with someone to make love.

"I was thinking about Demetri's?" He watched her get off the bed, and in her nakedness she walked toward the en-suite bathroom. It did not seem to bother her that he was watching.

"I recall where you keep everything in the kitchen. I will make myself a drink while I wait," he called out to her as he gathered up what clothes he had in the bedroom.

Turning on the water and stepping into the shower, she began to soap her body and wash her hair. With the water running, she did not hear the bathroom door open. Going to the night-side table to grab a condom, he undressed as he watched her in the shower, it was not long again before he had an erection, and he sheathed his rising cock.

She heard the shower door open, and she turned to find an anxiously erect Jack standing right behind her. Heated tension sparked again. He gave her a quick peck on the lips then turned her around again so that he was standing behind her. She was facing the inside wall of the stall with his cock pressed firmly against her ass. It was demanding attention. Her hands were on the shower walls to brace herself as he took his foot to spread her legs apart, his hand finding her wet, warm mound. His finger lingered, spreading her folds apart, tracing her swollen clit, and she let out moans of pleasure, calling his name. Still standing behind her, he lifted her leg up over his arm as he slammed his stiff cock into her hot and wet pussy. He moaned at his own pleasures as he slid in and out, pumping like a jackhammer, finger still rubbing her clit, her reflexes and twitching telling him that she just had her own orgasm. Then he came. She threw her head back against his shoulder as she gasped, "Uummmm." She reached behind her, running her hands up and down his firm thighs. Letting go of her, he stepped out, took off the condom, and tossed it into the garbage and dried off, and attempted to help her towel off…

"Thanks. I needed that." She snatched the towel that he was about to use. "I can manage to dry off by myself." What was with the attitude she was giving him? She enjoyed the sex, had never had it in the shower, but she wasn't in control. Could that have been it? She was confused. Sex with Jack was always good, but was it enough? She was trying to force herself to think of this relationship with Jack as more than just sex. He was looking for a genuine relationship. She still wasn't sure if that was what she wanted with him. What was Rick doing right now? Why had he been avoiding her?

They both got dressed and left for a late dinner at Demetri's. The place was packed, but they had a table in the back corner. It was unusually loud tonight, and Rick was invading her thoughts yet again. That can't be…*Just had mind-blowing sex with Jack.* Her thoughts were all over the place. Although the place was packed, their food arrived quickly. She was grateful. She was not really in the mood to have idle chitchat. *It's Jack who I'm here with here tonight. Concentrate, girl.* Forcing a smile across her lips, she bit into the juicy burger.

"I honestly don't know how you can eat that greasy thing and keep the figure that you have," he said to her as he gestured with his hand up from her head down to her feet.

"It works for me, I guess…I exercise, probably not as often as I should. Most of the time it's nothing but health drinks and salads with lots of water." She took another bite of her burger.

The music was slow and the lights had dimmed. He got up from his chair, extending his hand, requesting a dance. She hesitated a little, and, reluctantly, she stood and let him lead her to the dance floor, where he took her into his strong arms and guided her around the floor. He didn't try to impress her with moves. Their dance was a gentle, slow dance in rhythm to the music. Flashes caught her eyes. The paparazzi were here. *Damn. No peace, not even a quiet dinner.*

"Let's go. I've had enough." She looked up into his eyes, seeing that he was enjoying this attention. Being a photojournalist himself, he understood where they were coming from. It was sometimes the difference of bread and milk on the table to starving. He led her off the dance floor and tossed some cash onto their table as he grabbed their coats. She took the front of her coat to conceal her face somewhat. She noticed that he held out his arm to guard them from the paparazzi getting closer. He always knew how she preferred her exposure. They caught a cab back to her place and rolled around in bed a little more before finally falling asleep.

The sun was trying to shine its way through the bedroom drapes.

"Good morning, sunshine...How did you sleep?" he asked as he pulled himself up into a sitting position.

"How long did I sleep? It felt like we were up all night," she said in a laughing tone, looking at this handsome man who shared her bed and had wild, passionate sex with her for what seemed like all night. "Are you hungry?" she asked.

"Yeah, are you? Did you have a good time last night?"

"Yeah...Smart-ass..." she said, laughing and curling up under the blankets next to him, smelling his morning aroma that was made up of sweat and sex.

"You...want me to cook breakfast?" she managed to say while kissing this man.

"Never mind." And they started kissing again.

Minutes later, they broke for a breath of air and decided that it was time to get out of bed. They had plenty of things that they could to do this fine, crisp winter day. She suggested that they take a buggy ride through Central Park, and he agreed. Who knew what would happen next? It was during their trip through Central Park that she realized that she was beginning to have warm feelings. When did that happen, and what did they mean? She wanted to take things slow and easy, remember? Where did Rick fit into all of this? It had been a really long time since she felt this way, but she was still confused. Was she having these feelings for Jack or Rick? Could she tell Jack yet? No, that was not in the cards, even though she already knew his feelings, but why prolong the agony? What about Rick? Was that why she wanted to hold off?

Chapter Six

They started off just lounging around the apartment, doing whatever, from playing card games to tickling one another to sitting and watching movies on HBO. It was Amy who broke the silence.

"Jack…What do you think about me selling the penthouse? Now, before you say anything. I've given it a lot of thought, and I want to be near what family I have left, and that means moving back to Soul's Valley!"

He had this stunned look on his face. One that said he could not believe that she was asking for his opinion.

"Jack!" This huge grin came across his face, and he broke out into laughter.

"What's so funny?" she demanded.

"Your face, the reaction, everything! Amy, you asked me a question that really has no bearing on what I think. You said you were not ready for any type of commitment, and I respect that. But your question has insinuated otherwise! Do you really care as to what I think?"

"Yes…I enjoy being with you, around you. I'm not sure what type of relationship I'm looking for. My question was asking a friend his opinion, nothing more. Let's change the subject, then. Have you decided as to whether or not you are spending Christmas with me in Soul's Valley?" She had this way about her, that if she didn't get the response that she was really looking for, then she would change the subject.

"Yes…I would love to spend Christmas with you, wherever you may be!"

The subject of selling the penthouse did not arise again while they just sat around the apartment watching TV and having playful, fondling sex, making each other climax without even engaging in the act.

They ordered pizza, and again he was flabbergasted at the amount of food that she was able to consume and keep that fabulous, curvy figure. They talked more about her reasons for wanting to sell the condo, and her next assignment was to be a surprise, according to Sophie, who she still had to call. She reached for the phone and dialed Sophie's home number. They had that kind of agent-client relationship. Sophie was one of her best friends. It rang a couple of times before she answered it.

"Hello, darling, I was beginning to think that you were ignoring me…We've been sitting idle too long." She let out a little laughter.

"No, no, no…I'm not avoiding you, my dear. I just got back from the ranch. It's been hectic. So tell me more about this next surprise assignment you have for me."

"Well, before we head to Hawaii in March, I have a hair care line that has asked that you be their spokesmodel. They want to start production the week after New Year's!"

"That is awesome. It will give me some time to get reacquainted with my family again. Thanks, Soph." They chatted some more about the assignment and what each other was doing over the Christmas holidays, and then she hung up the phone and turned her attention back to a sleeping Jack. She didn't realize that she had been on the phone that long.

The next day they drove up together in Jack's car to the estate. There was idle conversation about anything and everything. Jack was a big Maple Leafs fan and was looking forward to seeing one of their games in the New Year. She talked about the ranch and the breeding process, and more recently that her father had started to race his thoroughbred horses. And how he had been training Autumn Fate for the Canadian Triple Crown. It was said that Fate's grandsire was

Galileo, who had won the Kentucky Derby multiple times. She also told him who most of the people were and what they looked like so that he wouldn't feel too uncomfortable. The drive didn't seem all that long this time as they drove up the driveway.

"Which way do I turn?" He shot her an inquisitive look as he approached the *Y* in the driveway.

"Keep to left. That will bring you to the garage beside the house."

Pulling the car up into place, he turned to her as he put it into park and shut off the engine. He didn't have to say anything. She knew what he wanted, so she leaned toward him. Their embrace started their embers of desire that had to be put on the back burner, for now, anyway. "Until later," he said as they broke. It is starting to fall into place, Jack thought to himself.

Rick saw the car come up the driveway, but he didn't recognize it, so he started up the drive to the house and stopped dead in his tracks when he saw Amy. She was home again, but not alone. Something stirred inside him. It was jealousy. He had no right to be jealous. They were not in any kind of relationship. Just because they slept together once, or should he rephrase that, shared the same bed, didn't mean she owed him anything. He saw them kiss. It ached, and it felt like his whole world was falling apart. It had to be love. He only ever felt this way once before with his wife Leanne, who passed away two years ago with H1N1 flu. He quickly turned around before they saw him. He had to get over her. That was all there was to it.

They tried to slide into the house unnoticed, but of course Joe was nearby and heard them enter.

"Good day, Miss Amy. Did you have a pleasant trip?" he inquired with a welcoming smile.

"Yes, I did, Joe…I would like to introduce to you my…Ah, this is my friend Jack Hayes." She introduced the two.

"Pleased to meet you, sir. May I take your bags upstairs, Mr. Hayes, Miss Amy?"

"Just plain ole Jack, please."

"Yes, to my old room please, Joe. Is there anyone around?" she asked, taking off her coat and reaching for Jack's to hang them up just behind the kitchen door.

"Miss Sandra and Andy are at the pool. Will there be anything else?"

"No, and thanks," she replied.

"Shall we start off right and take our things up to the room? Or would you like to grab a snack before dinner?" she asked, looking at Jack.

"Why don't we just go upstairs, unpack, and take a rest before I am tortured into meeting your family," he replied with a tone of sarcasm.

"Okay. Let's go…Upstairs, turn to your right…Two doors down to the left. Voila. Perhaps we should move to the guest room! I think that you will feel more comfortable there. At least until Anna can get these packed away for me." She was referring to all her dolls, just the way she had left them, on their shelves, one on the bed, and Susie Q standing by the closet.

"All right, if you say so. But I was looking forward to playing dolls with you. Shuck a darn," he said in a little boy's voice and kicked his foot across the floor, making a shuffling noise.

"Why you little pervert!" she called out to him as she ran out the door and up the hall.

"That's not fair, Amy. You know where to hide. Come back here, or I am not playing anymore," he called out to her. He listened very carefully, almost straining to hear her giggle. Just when he thought he knew where she was, he felt a tap on his back. He swung around on one foot to be face to face with whom he thought to be Amy.

"Now that is not fair, where did you come from? I could have sworn that I heard you over there!" He pointed in the opposite direction, not really paying any attention to her attire.

"I'll never tell how I got here, but I do think that there is someone that you should meet." A wet little boy stepped out from behind her.

"Andrew, I would like for you to meet…I'm sorry, but I just realized that I don't know you!" Sandra said in her normal tone of motherly voice. He came out around his mother, shyly at first, then piped in.

"Saint Nick will be here in this many more days…" He stuck out three small fingers.

"Three days? I thought that I had at least four more days before the big sleep." Jack lowered himself to the young boy's level.

"Yeah, four more days, that's what I said." Andrew tried again to hold out four fingers, still only showing three. Jack helped him with the fourth one. He stood again and turned his attention back to the situation on hand.

"You are not Amy…" He was astonished by the resemblance, same colour of hair, but this woman's eyes had a hint of gray-green, unlike the hazel-green of Amy's. He just stood there totally unaware that Amy was standing right behind him. If it weren't for the little boy putting his hand over his mouth to hide his giggles, he would never have turned around.

"Unbelievable…I cannot get over how much you two look alike, and you…" He looked right into Amy's green eyes. "That was a dirty trick!"

"Oh, Jack, lighten up a little. It was funny watching you. This is Sandra and Andy."

"Pleased to meet you, Jack…I'm sorry, but it just seemed appropriate at the time. We use to do that sort of thing when we were younger, when it was much more difficult to tell us apart," Sandra replied with an apologetic smile.

"No real harm done, anyway. I'm a grown boy, I think that I can handle this…I hope." He reached out to rub the top of Andrew's head as his eyes widened with a large smile directed back at Amy.

"What on earth were the two of you doing up there anyway, running from room to room?" Sandra asked as they sat down in the family room.

"I just thought it would be fun. It started out as a move from my room…too girlish for the big boy here. So I decided until my room is redecorated, we would just stay in the guest room. Then I remembered all the little tricks we used to play. I am sorry, Jack. It never dawned on me that I let it lapse that my sister is also my identical twin!"

He changed the conversation topic and turned his attention back to the young boy.

"It's a nice big house…A person could get lost here. Where is the pool that you two were enjoying so much?" Jack asked Andrew as he came over to where he was sitting in the chair, absorbing the information that Amy was telling him about her twin.

"On the other side of the house, where the hot room is," Andrew replied in a shy little voice, pointing to beyond the French doors.

"Would it be all right if I asked you to join me in another swim? Do you think your mom would object?" he asked the little tyke.

"No…But I better ask anyways. Mom, Mom, Mom…" He tugged at her pant leg, finally getting her attention.

"Yes, you may go with Jack…but mind your manners, listen to him. All right?"

"Okay, let go, Jack!" He grabbed his hand, trying to drag him along.

"So what's up, sis? You look happy one minute then lonely the next! Are things serious for the two of you?" Sandra asked her, waiting until the two boys were out of earshot with a look of concern on her face.

"Nothing is really the matter. I'm starting to get restless, just anxiously waiting for the next assignment to start, which is the first of the New Year. Working helps keep my mind off of things, like Daddy and Momma. I miss them. Is that funny or strange to you?"

"No, not at all. If it helps, they knew that you loved them. There were no hard feelings. They often spoke of how proud of you they were. I, on the other hand, still need to graduate from law school and to study for the bar exam. But everything has been put on hold. Philip didn't like the idea at first, wanted me to stay home and look after the family. Well, he got his wish. Andy will have a little brother or sister about July of next year."

"Sandi, I'm so happy for you. That explains the morning sickness and being tired all the time…Does anyone else know yet?"

"Ladies, can I start dinner now? Mr. Philip has arrived," Anna asked from the doorway.

"Yes…And, Anna, please send for Jack and Andrew to come and get ready for dinner. They're over at the pool. Thank you," replied Sandra.

"Philip doesn't know yet! I have had problems in the past, and if I make it over the first trimester the doctor says I should be able to carry to full term. So please, mum's the word." Sandra shot her a knowing look of concern and happiness over her recent condition.

She pretended to zip her mouth at the request of her sister. Just then Philip entered the room. Now she had a chance to look at this handsome gentleman that her sister married. He was tall, yet a little husky, with the darkest brown eyes that she ever saw, fair complexion—must be the Swedish side showing—darkest blond hair, and must be in his late thirties. Amy had this knack for guessing what origin people were.

"How was your day, dear?" Philip asked Sandra as he bent over to kiss his beautiful wife, but he could not help but notice how much the women looked alike.

"Just fine, dear. Look who's back from New York, and she brought a friend to stay over the holidays, too! And how was your day at the office?"

Looking back and forth between the two women, trying to figure out what they were up to. Both of them wore this devious look on their faces. They were up to something. He just knew it. "All right, the usual, you know the bickering. Jesus, it is the holidays, you would think that they could stop long enough to enjoy the festivities," he replied.

Chapter Seven

Philip was telling her about the new plans to breed Mystery with Sir Lancelot, the new stallion from Kentucky. Sir Lancelot had won plenty of races and showed great promise. With Rich's helping hand and the awesome job that he was doing, the girls were looking forward to fulfilling their father's dream of putting Mystical Ranch on the racing-circuit map. Amy was thinking that Philip was putting a lot of trust and competence into Rick's abilities. Just then, the boys came back into the room from their swim.

Jack came back downstairs after he had changed from his swim. "Boy, that was a great swim. You'll have to join me for another, Amy, after dinner. Am I starved."

Looking right at Philip, he extended his hand and introduced himself as Amy's boyfriend who was pleased to be here. He turned to look at her, and she had this annoyed look on her face.

She had yet to agree that they were boyfriend and girlfriend. Who was he to introduce himself to her family as that! Man, was she ever starting to get peeved and easily irritated. Maybe it was time to go back to work, or could it be that she was thinking of Rick? Was she sending Jack mixed signals? She needed to get a handle on this and figure out exactly what *this* was that she and Jack had. And what she wanted from whatever it was that she was calling it. As he was already thinking *this* was a relationship.

Jack had this look of familiarity, but Philip could not put his finger on it right now. Besides, he better be polite, or Sandra would never forgive him, at least until...*Who is he? I've seen him around before!*

"Pleased to make your acquaintance. So how long have you known our Amy?" Philip was acting like the big brother. He felt that he owed that much to Ivan. "I'm sorry, that is none of my business." *The hell it ain't.*

"That's all right, Phil. I can call you Phil, can't I? I met Amy in Paris, just after her divorce. We had a short relationship, parted, and found each other again. Didn't we, babe!" he replied, walking over to her, giving one of his most endearing smiles, and putting his damp arm around her shoulder.

"That pretty much sums it up. Shall we go in for dinner?" she responded with a little annoyance to her tone, waiting for Philip to lead the way. After all, he was the master of the house now that Daddy was gone.

They all sat down around the table, leaving the head of the table for the parents that had passed on. It was a lovely dinner, starting with either a fresh garden salad or the most appetizing French onion soup. To follow was a tender roast of beef with all the major fixings. After everyone had finished the main course, Anna came to clear the table, asking if anyone besides young Andrew wanted any dessert. She wasn't surprised with their reply of no-thank-yous, that it was a very delicious meal, but they were full. They indicated that they would take coffee and tea in the family room when it was ready. She obliged and brought out Andy's Jell-O Pudding Pops.

After dinner Amy had asked Anna to have her old room cleaned of the dolls, to just pack them away into the attic for now. Anna said she would get at it first thing the next day.

Gathered around to watch TV and relax until bed, they watched Christmas a special with Andrew. It was *Grandma Got Run Over by a Reindeer*. She hadn't seen this in years. It was one of her favourites, always managed to make her laugh. She was enjoying this quiet time with the family. She thought to herself that someday she hoped that she, too, would have a family and would be doing just this.

"Three more days…and Saint Nick comes. Did you know that, Aunt Amy?" Andrew asked, not knowing if she knew the answer, as he trotted over and climbed up onto her lap in the big comfy sofa. She put her arms around him.

"You are kidding, aren't you? I heard that he wasn't coming this year, that his elves had gone on vacation and he had no one to make the toys for all the kiddies," she replied in a soft, teasing tone, giving him a little squeeze. She remembered times like this with their father, and how he would tease them in the same manner.

"That's not true, Aunt Amy…Santa gets his toys from the toy store. Daddy told me so, last year!" he said, giggling as he slid off of her lap and on his way over to his mother.

It had been some time since she saw Jack. He said that he would be right back, but he hadn't returned. The show was over, the drive was long from New York, and she was getting tired anyway. She excused herself and went upstairs to their room to find him on the phone. She wasn't worried. It could be anyone, right? Besides, why was she getting suspicious? She undressed and climbed into bed to lay behind him. Just as she climbed in, he said good-bye and hung up the phone.

Back downstairs, Sandra also thought that it was time for her son to go off to bed and have her quiet time alone with her husband.

"Andrew, I think that it's time that you went to bed. Tomorrow's going to be a busy day. We need to be getting last-minute things done before Santa arrives. Say good night to Daddy," she said in a sweet voice to her little boy and placed him firmly down from her lap.

"Okay, Mommy, g'night, Daddy. Love you." He went over to his father to hug him good night before running upstairs. He acknowledged the boy's good night, giving his son a hug and an "I love you" back.

"Go on up and get into bed. I will be right there." She waited until Andrew was out of earshot. She turned to look at her husband, who still looked very distraught at that point into the night. This was the hour that she usually saw him starting to relax after a hard day at the office.

"What's the matter, honey? Did something else go wrong at work today? You look like you are in another world! Can I help?" she asked.

"Promise you won't say anything to Amy or get mad at me?" he replied, motioning her to sit on his lap.

"Promise. What can possibly be this disturbing?" She plunked her butt down on his welcoming lap.

"It's Jack…I have this feeling that I have seen him before." Shaking his head, he said, "He's trouble. I just know he is. If I could only remember where I've seen him before."

"You, too! Rick said the same thing to me earlier. He's sure that he saw his name in the papers but can't remember for what. He was sure it was rotten. And I just don't like him. He makes me feel uncomfortable. He reminds me of those fortune hunters. What are we going do about it, Phil?"

"Nothing, right yet! Let's wait until after the holidays. Maybe he'll go back and forget about your sister," he said, trying to hide his skepticism.

After she tucked their son into bed, Sandra and Philip continued to talk and cuddle on the big sofa into the wee hours of the morning. He had asked her what life was like as a twin and growing up here. She told him that it wasn't always fun and games despite the reputation that identical twins had. Ivan wasn't always as easygoing as he was in his later years. Finally they decided to go off to bed.

The next day Amy took Jack down to the stables to meet the horses and team down there. After about half an hour down there, she wasn't surprised when he told her that this wasn't his thing and was going back up to the house. He had no objections to her staying down here. He said he could amuse himself on the computer. He had brought some work with him that he could do. Perhaps he would go for a swim with Andrew. He gave her a peck on the cheek and left.

She wandered around the stables, watching the men and women work with the horses. Rick's voice drew her attention in his direction. She watched as he showed Felix how to do something a few steps away. He captivated her attention, his strong muscles working hard lifting bales of hay into the stalls, his hamstrings tight as he bent from the waist down to pick them up. She was getting herself all hot and bothered just watching this fascinating man who was stealing her heart. Wait a minute, wasn't she here with Jack? She wasn't supposed to be thinking about Rick, but she couldn't help it. He had her mind in a prison at night, just remembering that one night of heated passion in his kisses. They never had sex.

She found herself standing mere inches from him in the stable. He was alone…From the heat that her body generated, he felt her standing behind him, and in one quick swoop, he had her lying next to him on the hay, out of sight of prying eyes. She let out a little, quiet yelp of playful pleasure.

"Hey there…How have things been going? Sandra tells me that you will be moving back here," he said, still holding her in his arms. She was a perfect fit. She had to have an idea of the kind of power that she had over him.

"Hey there yourself. It's going as good as it can, I guess. Sandra talks a lot. I see that nothing has really changed." She laughed softly so that no one could hear her. She had to be honest with him. "Hmmm, Rick, this feels so right to be in your arms. Why have you been avoiding me?" she murmured, not realizing that it was loud enough for him to hear as she snuggled her head against his chest.

He lifted her chin so that he could look down deep into her eyes before he spoke. "Cause if I didn't, I wouldn't be able to stop myself." He left it at that, and without saying another word between them, he took possession of her mouth with his, slowly at first, almost waiting to see if she rejected his advances. She didn't. Instead, she enveloped him into her own embrace, kissing him back with passion that had been pent up from their first encounter. Her hands roamed his back, rubbing, smoothing, caressing as they found his ass. She gave it a little squeeze. He let out a little "oh" as he opened his eyes in surprise at her affection. He took her face into his hands as he continued to kiss her with the same passion.

She broke away, scrambling quickly to her feet, mumbling something as she ran off, leaving him there stunned, wondering what on earth he had done. He thought that things were going okay, better than okay.

She was running so fast that she had to stop to catch her breath. She didn't run to the house. She found herself standing over their gravesite. A comforting feeling overwhelmed her. Why did she end up here? *Daddy, Momma…I miss you guys terribly. I need guidance. I am so torn. I am in love with Rick, yet I have invited Jack here. I don't know why I did that. I suggested that I would try to make things work with Jack, yet I keep finding myself drawn to Rick. Daddy, you have always known what is best for me. I really need some direction or a sign.* Nothing happened. There almost always was an immediate sign in the movies! But this was not the movies, this was her life. A complete, utter mess! She headed back toward the house. It was getting close to dinnertime, and she was sure that Jack would be looking for her.

This is going to be a long couple of weeks, to wait out the commercial production for that hair care product. What on earth am I doing? I am playing with fire, two men. Damn you, Rick! she spoke softly to herself as she walked toward the house.

Dinner was an unusual, quiet scene that night, just "pass the peas," "thank-yous," et cetera at the table. Yet they all gathered into the family room again to watch TV and read.

She talked with Jack after dinner in their room, trying to get some sense of feeling that would resemble a relationship and not just sex. She tried to get more information about his articles that he wrote. He would not comply on that, just told her that if he did his pen name would be compromised. So she just left it at that, and they turned in early, giving just quick little pecks for kisses. She was glad that she didn't have to have sex with him tonight. Her mind was still back at the stables with Rick and his kisses, his hands on her face. She could still feel the warmth and the passion on her cheeks.

She woke to having lights flashing in her eyes. When she stopped seeing stars, she saw Jack kneeling before her, taking pictures of her naked body.

"What the hell do you think you are doing!" She was stunned as she grabbed the blankets to cover herself. She liked posing for the camera, but with her clothes on. Nude pictures had their way of getting into the wrong hands. She was a little peeved.

"Relax, baby. I just wanted a little scrapbook with my beautiful woman in it. I swear these are for my eyes and mine alone. So just lay back and do what comes natural…Make love to my camera. Please!" he pleaded with that sexy, devilish smile that got him most of the time what he wanted.

She was having a hard time saying no to him. Was it because she wanted or needed this relationship to work? Was she being naïve? She didn't protest anymore, and she did what came naturally to her. Throwing back the covers, she delivered her flawless, golden-brown yet smooth-as-silk body, teasing the camera by gently covering up her boobs with one arm, sensuously letting a nipple peek through, and with the other slowly sliding, gliding her hand over her body. She almost brought herself to a climax, as she was creating this sensual desire, making herself hot…

Chapter Eight

"Oh god…Jack…I need you. *Now*. I've never done this before, it's soooo…hot. Take me, please…" she requested as she put her index finger into her mouth, her tongue running circles over it, sucking on it, pulling it in and out, tracing her bottom lip as her other hand slid down between her legs, opening them for his view, as she started to rub her swollen nub ever so gently. She started to pant. Her breathing was restless, her chest rose and fell with the anticipation accumulated within her.

He put the camera down and went to her on command, undressing. She could plainly see his erection. He immediately took her in his arms. He kissed her hot, sweet lips, slipping his excited tongue into her mouth. Slowly caressed her back, moving his hand to the front to massage her tits, kissing down her neck, now taking her erect nipple into his mouth, suckling ever so gently. The sensation sent shivers of desire through her like nothing else before. She took her hand and placed it on his erection, stroking it back and forth, rubbing her thumb over the head and slit. Jack whispered softly into her ear that he found her so sexy like this, his breathing erratic with desire and anticipation of what lay ahead of them. He laid her back down on the mattress, spreading her legs wide so that he could enter. Their wild sex intimacies went on like this for what seemed like hours. Suddenly, he was startled by the knocking on the door. He quickly grabbed the camera and slid it under the bed, out of sight, as he called to the door.

"Are you still in bed? I thought that Amy would like to go for a horse ride with me. It's a beautiful, warm winter morning," Sandra asked through the door.

"Sure, can you give me about half an hour to get ready, though?" Amy called back, slightly out of breath.

"No problem. Meet you downstairs in the dining room. G'morning, Jack!"

"Morning," he replied, thinking that was close, and what a way to ruin a romantic moment.

He already knew that he was not going to like living or staying here with the interruptions to come.

"Do you mind?" she asked as she climbed out of bed, heading for the en suite bath.

"No, no…Go ahead. I want to go into the city and get more film for tomorrow anyway. I might also stop by the office to see what my next assignment is going to be. You have fun. Okay. See you later. Love ya," he said as he jumped out of bed and back into his jeans, walking over to the chest of drawers to shut off the video camera that she was not aware of. He took the tape out and put it away into his suitcase for safekeeping.

He continued to get dressed. He was just finishing when she came out of the shower. He stood at the bathroom doorway and watched her as she toweled off. He hated himself for what he was about to do. This woman was the best thing that ever happened to him. He was beginning to have doubts about the pictures, but he needed the money. He had promised *Gentleman's Hardcore* magazine that he could deliver "nudes" of the world's top model, Amy Gordon. He knew that she kept her maiden name for personal reasons. The hardest part was getting her to agree to have the pictures submitted.

"Well, babe, I better go and let you visit. Have fun riding. I promise, I won't be long."

"Okay, see you later, stay out of trouble," she said, blowing him a kiss.

Amy finished getting ready in record time and still had time to spare, just enough to get her butt downstairs. This was going to be fun, riding with Sandra again. How she missed those lazy days riding in the meadow. There was no one in the dining room. Where was Sandi? Just then Anna came in.

"Where's Sandra, she said meet her here?" she asked.

"Sorry. Miss Amy, your sister received a call and asked that you meet her down at the stables, that she wouldn't be long."

After grabbing some toast from the breakfast bar, she took her coat and walked through the kitchen into the passage that led to the stables. She was not surprised to find Rick getting the horses ready for their ride. She just stood back to admire him for a moment, reminded of how her attraction to two men was creating such conflict. This was what brought her such difficulties, why she needed to get away from here again, away from Jack, too. She was so confused. She cleared her throat so that she was heard.

"Amy…I heard your breathing. Sorry, I have it memorized! You're staring at me. Why?" he inquired.

She was pretty much all he could think about after her little fall and the other little incidents that they kept having. Their hot kisses had him wanting more from her. He wanted to take her again, back to his bunkhouse with no interruptions, take her and make her his with passionate lovemaking. What would it be like with her? He did not plan on having these feelings again. He thought after his wife had died that he would never feel this way again.

"No particular reason. Listen, I need to apologize for my behavior the other day, it was uncalled for, not professional…" He was standing right in front of her, in her personal space again before she could finish. He did that a lot lately. She was having a hard time breathing normally. His mouth came at her with a force of desire that has been burning inside him. Amy had this way about her that had men desiring her. With Rick it wasn't her beauty and had nothing to do with her wealth. She just made him feel alive again.

She pulled away, breathless, still trying to catch her breath as she stood there before him, wanting him to kiss her again.

"Why do you keep pulling away from me? Have I done something to put you off?"

Shaking his head, all those pent-up feelings and desires stirring inside him, he continued, "You have to know what you do to me. You have awoken these feelings and desires that I thought were long gone…"

She was shocked to hear that he did feel the same way about her as she did about him. *Oh, God, what am I going to do now? I can't continue with Jack, not when I'm having such strong feelings for Rick.* Thoughts were going through her mind as the intercom came on…

"Rick…Rick, please tell Amy that I'm sorry, but something has come up and I can't go for that ride that we planned. Thanks."

"Well, you heard. Let me take you out for that ride? I think that we really need to talk about these things that are happening between us. Please?" he asked with a puppy-dog look in his eyes that she just could not refuse. It was a playful look, and besides, she wanted to be alone with him again. Maybe he would take her in his arms again and kiss her!

"All right…I agree that we need to talk about these things. Let's go out by the meadow."

Rick helped her mount the golden-brown stallion that they called Fate while he rode Mystery. They walked the horses side by side, bringing them to a gallop, then slowing them down again. For two people that shared wild, passionate kisses, they exchanged casual conversation while they rode. He told her his dreams for Mystical Ranch. She asked if he wanted his own someday, and he did, but for right now this was where he needed to be. He had a great crew working with him and he liked being here.

He lagged behind at times to catch a glimpse of her as she rode Fate, her body swaying with the movement of the horse. He wanted her but wasn't sure if telling her was the right thing to do.

Amy couldn't stop thinking about the night that she spent in his arms or the other times they were together while they were riding. He was awakening desires in her that she was not aware of. It was magic. She didn't feel this way when she was with Jack. There were no similarities to compare the two men. But if she had to compare the two to make a "pros and cons" list it would be something like:

Rick was sexier than Jack. She believed that he would also be a gentler, more passionate lover. Jack was rough with his lovemaking, but he made her explore new ways that she wouldn't do on her own. Like earlier that morning with the camera. She made love to it. She couldn't do that with Rick, or at least she didn't think so. She surprised herself by thinking that, realizing that she actually enjoyed this morning's stint. She was not ashamed of her body. It had taken her a long time to get to that point. She was torn between the two. Maybe she wasn't ready for a serious relationship. She wanted Rick, yet she wanted Jack. How many more men could she want?

They reached the meadow. It was a wide and open space surrounded by tall, beautiful pine and cedar trees, with a little pond in the middle that had a really thin layer of ice on it. It had one big oak tree that shaded the one corner. He jumped down to tie off the horses, and he helped her down. She sat down at the bench, and he sat next to her, taking her hand in his.

He turned to look into her face, almost lost for words. He had to have her in every sense of the word. His passion overcame him. He took her into his arms again, and, without saying a word, holding her head between his hands, he placed a hot, wanting kiss against her lips. It did not take her long to respond. Her arms embraced him, not wanting to let go, and she felt her whole body go warm. Her mind was going fuzzy with desire. He broke away this time, holding her back…

"Amy…" Silence overtook the moment briefly. "Please forgive me for what I'm about to say. It comes directly from my heart. I'm in love with you! I love the way you smile, your laugh. I feel your hurt, and I just want to make it all go away. I love the way you look when you're sleeping. The way you care about people around you. And…There are just so many more things that I love about you…" Before he could get another word out, she started in.

"Rick…I'm in love with you, too! The other night I haven't been able to forget, you have taken my thoughts prisoner. I'm so confused. I'm trying to be honest. I'm not in love with Jack…"

Amy startled herself with that one. She didn't realize it until now, but she didn't love Jack. Sex was great, but she thought about it, that was all she was attracted to. How could she tell him, on the day of Christmas Eve? She couldn't, it would have to wait until after Christmas. They were not going to work out.

He broke into her thoughts.

"Do you mean it's not serious with Jack Hayes?" he asked with a look, so serious again. Still facing him, she looked into his eyes with a passion that he saw every time that they were alone. The same look they shared from their first night together in his bed, although they were fully clothed. There was still a heated desire between them. The same passionate look that said that sex was not needed to feel the warmth of their love.

"Yes, I didn't realize until now that I want to be with you, but I can't tell Jack until after the holidays—Christmas, anyway. Can you wait that long? Then I promise we will work everything else out."

"I can wait that long. I've waited the past few months just to hear you say that you love me. I have something else that I need to say that I think that you should know about Mr. Hayes. It's not pretty, so there is no other way of putting it but bluntly. I just realized where I have seen him. He is the same guy that my cousin Carey was telling my mother about how he seduced her and other women. He also photographs them. Then he sells the pictures to those smut magazines. The trauma that he put her through, the reporters wouldn't leave her alone. I don't want this to happen to you. I love you, Amy."

There went that *L* word again. They both had said it today. Did she mean it? Yes, but it also scared the hell out of her. She already had one failed marriage. He had this passion about him she never saw in another man except her father.

Chapter Nine

The look in her eyes gave away what he'd already feared, that he'd already seduced her and took pictures. "When did it happen, where are the pictures?" he asked apologetically, taking her back into his arms and wanting to make the hurt go away.

"What do you mean? What makes you so sure that he has pictures of me?" she asked.

She lifted her head slightly up to look into the eyes that felt her hurt and anger yet were so full of compassion. She knew then that she wanted Rick for the rest of her life.

"Amy…" He paused to catch his breath in the cool air. "I think that I know you well enough to know when you are trying to hide something. Your face says it all. We may have known each other only a few months, but it feels like a lifetime. Please don't hide it from me. I'm here to help in any way that I can."

"I have this feeling that they are the reason he went to the city, to get the roll he took this morning developed! Wouldn't he have to know someone to get that type of pictures developed?" she said, feeling sorry for herself for letting this man get to her, trying so hard to be strong and not let the tears come. Jack was someone she thought she had cared about.

"Wait a minute. He'll be able to get them developed at just about any of the photographers' studios in the city. What if they believe in any lie that he would tell? Oh, my God! Rick, what am I going to do? It could ruin my career if those pictures get out!" she exclaimed. She felt a tear start to run down her cheek just as Rick saw it, and he gently wiped it away with his thumb.

"Slow down, one problem at a time! Let's see if he brings them back tonight. Ask him to show them to you then confront him with his intentions."

She agreed to his suggestion. They kissed and just sat there for a few moments longer and held each other, and then they mounted their horses and rode back to the stables. It was a much quieter ride. They were both thinking about the same thing, Jack Hayes and what he thought he was going to get away with. Watching him brush the horse down after their ride was a very arousing action to her, the way that his hand stroked the horse's mane. She wanted it to be her mane that he was combing. She walked around Fate, took the brush from him, and started to back him into the stall, where no one could see them. She playfully put her leg behind him to trip him back onto the haystack. Laughing, she came down on him. She took possession of his mouth in one smooth swoop. Her body pressed firmly against his, and it wasn't long before she felt his attraction to her.

He broke their kiss briefly. "You have to know what you do to me! Unless you are prepared for what can come next, I suggest that we…oh, hell, woman."

He took what was being offered to him. Hands were roaming, touching places that were forbidden before. Her warm skin under his touch was becoming much more arousing with every inch he touched.

Amy disengaged herself from him by taking a step up. She stopped herself before they did get carried away. "You're right. I need to first get things cleaned up with Jack." She reached for his hand to help him up and placed a soft peck on his cheek as she wrapped her arms around him before she left for the house.

Meanwhile, back at the house, Jack had returned from the city, earlier that he really planned. He went upstairs to their room. He had taken the roll of film into a buddy's studio to develop, anxious to see the pictures. To see if any were good enough to send to his contact at *Gentleman's Hardcore*. He picked up his suitcase and put the pictures away for the time being. He needed a plan to convince her that they were awesome and that she should do a photo shoot for one of the porn mags. That although he had her to himself, he wouldn't feel offended to share her beauty with the rest of the male population. That it would be a fantastic opportunity for her career.

Again hoping that Amy would approve, he didn't want to resort to forging her name, although his friend was getting pretty good at it. He had another big problem. He was falling in love with her. Those pictures were his only way out of debt. The money that he was going to collect on those was enormous. I'll show her the pictures later, convince her that they are for our purposes, and just maybe hint that they are good enough for… He was speaking out loud again.

Rick told her to act like nothing had happened, to play it cool, once they were back at the house. So she went up to the house, where it seemed empty. Where was everyone? she thought. She decided to go take a long swim to relax before dinner when she ran into Sandra in the hallway.

"I thought everyone was gone! Where did you go? You missed a great, refreshing ride," Amy said, grinning from ear to ear, which Sandra noticed immediately.

"I know, but Philip called and needed some papers that he forgot on his desk. I had to run them into town. And I just tucked Andrew in for his afternoon nap before dinner. Did you ride by yourself, or did ya have some company, like, perhaps, a guy by the name of Rick?" Sandi asked with a hint of mischief.

"Now, now, Sandi, you know that I'm trying to be serious about Jack. Why would I go riding with Rick?" She was trying to keep her face straight and serious. She hoped that her twin couldn't tell she was hiding something, yet she wore this big grin that was impossible to hide.

"Amy, Amy, you cannot tell a lie. You never have been able to. Your eyes are your tattletales. I know about yours and Rick's night of heated passion. I mean, you didn't come back that night of Dad's funeral until early morning. Plus I see it every time that you return from the stables, you have this 'I just got lucky' expression written all over your face, plus you have this glow that we tend to get when we are in love. Just admit that you have a thing for Rick and I will leave you alone!" Sandra said with a bit of sarcasm in her voice.

She was a little shocked at what her sister had said, but she only spoke what she thought was the truth. What was she going to say now? One failed marriage, a bad relationship with a pervert. In love again, with the ranch manager. Was it déjà vu all over again? What on earth was she going to do? She'd better say something, or Sandi would never shut up, and with her luck that would be when Jack walks in.

"Sandi…You are my beloved sister. What can I say, except that you are only partially right." Looking around to make sure that there was no one around to hear, she continued. "I went riding with Rick. I realized a few things about my life. We've kissed, in fact we have kissed a number of times. I feel connected to him. There's this connection that we share. I don't know what to do. We held each other that night I bumped my head, but we did not, I repeat myself, we did not make love that night, nor did we have sex, just to clarify that for you. We have yet to have sex. I keep pulling back, something is not yet right! I don't know if it's this thing that I have going with Jack! Today he told me a few things about Jack that I didn't know," she was telling her sister in a whisper.

"So what are we going to do?" Amy said as she noticed Jack coming toward the room. "Talk about it later, all right. I don't want Philip to find out yet," Sandi replied, trying to cover up their conversation with something else.

"Yeah, all right. At the same time, we should go through some of Daddy's things."

He knew the girls were talking about something that they didn't want anyone else to hear. He just wasn't sure what it was. Jack wasn't stupid.

Amy caught Sandi's impromptu. She quickly turned to him.

"So, Jack, did you get a chance to go and see about your new assignment? Any ideas what it will be?" Amy asked, trying to break the tension in the room that one could cut with a knife as she also leaned into him to give a quick peck on his cheek.

"No, I never got the chance. I ran into an old friend in the city, you might know him…Steve Landers. He's into the stock market now, made a killing last year. We went over to the pool hall, drank a few, and shot some balls. How was your ride, babe?" he asked so casually. He was well aware of the looks that Sandra was shooting in his direction. He was also aware that most of the people in this house didn't like him very much, it was almost mutual. It wasn't that anyone was rude. He just picked up on the tension when he was around. He was also sensing something else with Sandra and Amy, but he could not put his finger on it. It could be nothing. The two hadn't seen each other in quite some time and had a lot of catching up to do, and apparently a lot of personal items to go through of their parents'.

"The ride was good. It was refreshing and felt good to be on Fate again. I have missed riding. It has been way too long. If no one has any objections, though, the nap that Andrew is taking sounds very appealing. Think I'll go up and take one, too. So please excuse me," she said, trying to sound more tired than she really was.

Jack never suspected that she had other motives for going up to their room. She entered the room to find his suitcase on the bed. Puzzled, she turned to lock the door. She didn't want to be disturbed, as she was going through the room until she found the pictures.

They had to be here! She started in the most obvious place, the suitcase. Trying not to disturb anything, she found them. Looking at them, she had to admire herself. Hmmm maybe I should submit them, no, better idea yet, I'll arrange to have their photographer do them, tastefully, and screw up his plans. That ought to teach him a lesson or two. This should be interesting, she whispered to herself.

Chapter Ten

She called Rick and talked to him about her plans, and he agreed that it was a good idea, but he also made her promise to get the existing pictures and negatives away from him. He supported any decision that she made. She told him how much she enjoyed their little escapade this afternoon and could not wait to see him again. In fact, they discussed her coming down to the office so that they could continue the conversation. She told him that she liked his way of thinking but felt that it might be just a little undoable, being that Sandra was home and Amy wasn't sure how she would get out of the bedroom unnoticed. So they agreed that they could wait to see each other tomorrow. She was glad that things were out in the open with them.

He was starting to feel regret. He wanted Amy in every possible way, and he knew that he also had to tell her the truth about himself, which was one of the smaller reasons that he wanted her to come down to the office. It was the first time in his life that he felt that he had been living a lie. He understood the consequences that would revolve around him telling Amy about his family and the witness protection program that they were placed into nearly twenty years ago.

To him, it was really only his name that was a lie. His schooling and the fact that he had been married before were real facts. It was everything else about his family and his parents' life that was fictitious. His brothers and sister led pretty much normal lives, as normal as they could in the program. They only had to endure losing their names, and their parents lost everything they had worked so hard for. But his father continued to his dying days to say that he did the right thing in turning in the evidence that convicted Sontiago. His mother said that she would not have changed a thing about his father, that she would always respect his decision to protect his family. He watched his father endure the heartaches of losing his own parents and not being able to be there for them. His mother now lived in British Columbia, his two brothers were still in Alberta, and his sister had moved to Australia. They were all happy and content with their lives.

Philip was working in the study. Although his office was now officially closed for the holidays, he still had a heavy workload and promised that he would be home for the holidays, but he needed to get most of this cleaned up before the New Year came in. The project depended on it. Sandra understood and rarely interrupted him when he worked from home, but this was family and was important. She had to talk to him about Jack and what she had learned this afternoon after talking with Rick earlier.

She knocked on the office door and opened it just a crack. "Hey, honey, can I interrupt you for a few minutes? We need to have a little powwow," she said, as she didn't bother to wait for a response and entered the room, turning to close the door so that prying ears could not hear them.

"Sure? What's up?" He adored his beautiful wife. He was noticing some small changes in her appearance lately but still loved her dearly. "Come here and sit on Poppa's lap, I have missed you today." He patted his lap for her to come over as he also pushed his chair away from the desk.

She sauntered her way over and sat down as instructed. "I spoke with Rick earlier. We had a nice conversation about our houseguest. He remembered where he heard the name before…And apparently he has already told Amy. I need to go upstairs and talk with her, see how she is handling this and what direction she wants to take. Hopefully, he won't be around much longer." She recited the details of Jack's past from her conversation with Rick earlier. She got up to go and chat with Amy. Before doing so, she planted a loving kiss on his lips, leaving a taste for more to come, leaving him speechless for a few seconds.

"Hey, hon..." He rose from his chair and walked toward his wife before she reached the office door. "Everything is going to be okay. Chin up. Love you!" He gave her a loving hug before letting her go.

She was kicking herself in the behind. Amy could not believe how she could have been so blind about Jack! Was she just so sex crazed that she would have sex with anyone that turned her on? No, that couldn't be true, either. Rick turned her on big time, but she managed to keep pushing him away. She had good sex before. Jack was a so-so lover. He only did things that he felt would benefit himself when it came to pleasure. But he took her places that none of the others had. Wasn't that just what she had been thinking earlier?

Now, Rick was a whole new playing field. That scene in the stable! She really could have gotten things heated up there. It would not have taken her long to be persuaded to do the cowboy hustle. Okay, now she was scaring herself. What was she becoming, a sex-craving maniac? No, what she felt for Rick was definitely more than just that. She never just spent a night with a guy, sharing the same bed, not having sex, and walked away the next morning. She could still feel the passion, the desire to just be near him, to feel those protecting arms around her, to know that he wanted to make everything in her world okay. He was someone that she could see spending the rest of her life with, sharing her hopes and dreams with. This was what her parents had. This was what she had been holding out for.

After she finished talking to Rick, she thought she better put the pictures back. In doing so, she stumbled across a videotape. Now what? She took the tape out and went over to the video recorder to watch. After seeing the light about the true Jack Hayes, she didn't put a single thing past him. She watched in awe. Jack with other women in bed. This was disgusting. How many were there? Fast-forwarding the tape, she stopped when this woman caught her eye. It was her! It was this morning's little tryst. How dare he! What was he planning, blackmail? Taking the tape out, she decided to hide it. He wouldn't be able to ask about it because she was not to know about it. *He has to go!* Quickly hiding the tape and putting the suitcase down on the floor, unlocking the door, and climbing into bed, she heard someone coming down the hall.

"Knock knock, may I come in?" Sandra asked.

"Sure, come on in." Sitting on the bed, she instructed Sandra to lock the door before joining her on the bed. Sandra gave her a queer look. "What gives, sis? First you're whispering, now we are behind locked doors?"

Sandra wanted her to confide in her, although she already knew about most of it from talking to Rick.

Amy showed Sandra the tape, shaking the tape in her hand. It was too vulgar to play otherwise. They discussed her plans to ruin Jack. Sandra was on board with the idea. Sandra told her about Philip's and her own suspicions about Jack, and how they had already talked with Rick, who in turn had told them everything, including about the pictures, so it came as no surprise that he had a videotape of them. What a creep. There was total silence for a while in the room. Sandra reached out and embraced her sister, giving a firm yet caring hug to help ease the pain that had been inflicted on her. Being identical twins, Sandra sensed that something terrible was happening in her sister's life long before she had talked to Rick earlier.

"What can I do to help you? We all want to help in any way that we can, and we support your decisions one hundred and ten percent. As for the nude thing, are you sure that it won't hurt your career and that it is something that you want to do?" Sandra said in soft, caring tones that made her the best sister ever.

"Sandi, after I saw the pictures, I had this revelation. I am at the point in my career that it doesn't matter. I am already considered the world's top model, have been for a couple of years. So I go out with a bang! It's time to start something new. Who knows, maybe it will be at Rick's side?" The last statement surprised them both. She admitted it. Rick meant a lot to her. She wanted him in her life going forward.

Sandra couldn't leave that last statement alone. "So when did you realize that Rick was the one?"

"I've been fooling myself. Every time that we are alone, this heat of passion and desire just sweeps over me…These past couple of days, before this thing with Jack came to a head, Rick has been invading my thoughts day and night. I just had a wild thought. Want to do me a favour?" She could not help but smile just thinking about Rick and the plan that she just thought of.

Sandi saw this as she let go of her sister. She was happy to see that Amy had finally found someone that would make her happy. She already knew how Rick felt about her sister. They had their own little talks during the day, little hints that he dropped around, asking about her, just about every time he saw her, before Amy returned home to the ranch.

"You know that I would do just about anything for you. What are you thinking?" Seeing that devilish look in her sister's eyes, she already guessed what she was up to before she said it.

"I need to go and see Rick. It's just this urge that I need to see him. I was thinking about how to get me out of the house without Jack seeing me. Trade me places for an hour? Let me be you to get out," she confided in her older sister.

"Ames, it's crazy, but I will help you. Here, put these on, then I will go and change into something else," she said as she started to strip to give her sister her clothes. This was just like when they were teens.

They talked a bit more about the events of the day as they exchanged clothes for this little tryst that Amy was embarking on. She admitted that she did not love Jack, that she was in love with Rick. He had made her realize things about herself that she didn't know existed.

She decided as she ran down to the stables that she couldn't wait any longer. Tonight had to be the night. It was time to confront Jack about these, to call everyone to the family room after dinner.

After a short search, she found Rick standing outside overlooking the ranch, something that he often did when he wanted to think.

Rick felt her standing behind him.

"Ames, you're here?" He spoke as he swung around on his heels. "Don't get me wrong, I am always happy to see you, but we just spoke on the phone." He tipped his Stetson up to look at her.

"I know, but I just had to come down and see you, to feel your arms around me. Hold me, Rick," she said as she stepped closer to the man that she now knew that she loved. He took her into his arms. She felt good, but she was shaking.

"What's the matter, you are shaking like a leaf." He held her tighter.

"I'm just mad and furious with myself for letting him talk me into taking him back. I need to confess something…I have not been able to stop thinking about you. Even when I left for Milan, you were there with me." She looked up at him as he continued to hold her. "I knew even when I was kissing him that I wished it was you I was kissing." She let out a little giggle.

"Ahh, shucks, doll…I'll tell you again, you have invaded my thoughts since the night that you came home for your dad's funeral. And I *do love you*!" He lifted her chin so that he could kiss her, something that he had longed to do again and again. He broke their kiss to tell her, "I want to share everything with you. I have fantasies of you." It wasn't the right time to tell her about his past. This was about her problems with Jack.

They talked some more and kissed a few more times before he gave her a big hug. She asked him to be there by her side when she confronted Jack tonight, and he was thrilled that she wanted him there and told her so, and then they left to go up to the house. She felt better after being with Rick and actually talking to him face to face about this big mess and what his plans were for their ranch. And bringing her father's dreams to life of being the best thoroughbred racehorse ranch this side of the Great Lakes.

He knew that even though the girls had been apart for a number of years, since her coming back to the ranch, Amy had been confiding in Sandra. So he knew that he had Sandra's support and admiration for wanting to help protect Amy from this idiot that called himself her "boyfriend."

Anna called them to dinner. Amy had told Sandra earlier that she really didn't want anything to eat, that she was too furious to think about food. Jack inquired about Amy's absence from the dinner table. Sandra covered for her and said that she had a migraine and was resting for an hour or so. That seemed to satisfy him for the time being, but he still knew that the girls were up to something. He tried again to make small talk with Philip over dinner, but it appeared that everyone was in a little bit of a foul mood this evening.

It was after dinner when Amy and Rick returned to the house from the barn. Amy asked Rick to wait in the kitchen for her while she went upstairs to get the evidence that they needed to confront Jack. She came back downstairs and met Rick, and then they walked together into the family room. She thought that she would be able to control her anger and emotions once she saw Jack, but she was sadly mistaken. Her blood was boiling at this point, and she could not control it any longer. She walked into the room toward him, screaming and waving the pictures.

"How dare you! What on earth were you thinking, Jack! This could ruin my career. Did you stop to think about that? You probably did. And this…" She gave it a second thought, deciding not to hand over the videotape to him but to Philip instead. "You are perverted, sick, and a few other words I won't mention, because I'm a lady. I would like for you leave my home! We are through." Standing there staring through him, as if she saw him for the first time, he disgusted her. She was still kicking herself in the ass for listening to him back at her apartment.

"You are not giving me a chance to explain myself. Ready to convict before giving me the chance to prove myself innocent. Counselor over there"—he pointed to Sandra—"knows that I have rights to a fair trial. Just hear me out, let me explain…" He was cut short.

"Why? So that you can tell me more lies? Forget it. It ends here." She turned her back on him, moving to stand beside Rick, who put his arm around her to let her know that he was there for her, and Philip, who just stood there in awe over her strong stance. She really was Ivan's daughter. He only ever saw that man get that riled up once.

"Amy, would it make any difference if I told you that it was different with you. That I really do love you! I didn't want to hurt you. Please give us another chance." He was pleading.

"No! *You know why*? 'Cause I found out about your sick little games. You prey on women and use them. I can't press charges, because you haven't done anything to me, but I can give this tape"—she pointed to the videotape that Philip now held—"to the police, and *I am* sure they will be able to do something about it. I really do think that you have overstayed your welcome. I'll ask again, politely. Please leave now. You will find your suitcase by the kitchen door."

This really did throw a curve into his plans, but he knew enough to leave. He would have to think about this for a few days to see what to do next. He left and everyone watched as he drove away. She let her shoulders relax under Rick's arm. The tension was starting to leave her body.

"Phew, glad that is over. I can't believe he is such a slimeball. I believed everything that he said to me. What does that say about me?"

She placed her hand over her forehead, rubbing it while thinking…

"Honey, it doesn't make you a bad person. You're right about one thing. He *is* a slimeball! Don't do this to yourself. Let's move on. But as a lawyer, I would like to suggest that you make a formal complaint with the police," Sandra said as she walked over to give her another sisterly hug.

"One other thing left to do, call Sophie and have her arrange to have the photo shoot done before Jack has the opportunity to move forward." She called Sophie that night to explain everything to her after she did as Sandra suggested and called the police to make a formal complaint regarding Jack. She was flabbergasted with Jack and the thought that he would get away with it. Thankfully, the publishing world didn't really take holidays.

Like she said earlier to Sandra, it was time to move forward and what a better way to go out with a bang. She had the pictures but wasn't sure if that included the negatives.

Sandra announced that she still had gifts to wrap for Andrew before Santa came. So everyone scattered. Amy walked Rick to the back door, and they shared an intimate kiss before he left her for the night. She then went up to her room. She lay there thinking of the day's events, and thoughts of Rick filled her mind. She was too wound up to sleep. It had to be early Christmas morning. Thoughts of him just kept filling her up, making her feel warm all over. She was about to roll over and for the umpteenth time try for some sleep when there was a knock at the door. She turned to look at the clock. It was 5:30 a.m.

"Are you awake?" a voice whispered as he opened the door just a crack.

"Yes, come in, Rick," she replied. She recognized his soft, masculine voice.

"How did you ever guess? Never mind, I know the answer. I just wanted to be the first to wish you a merry Christmas, and I couldn't sleep anymore. Can I come over and give you a Christmas kiss?" he asked. What a gentleman, she thought.

"Please do. And back at you, I know that I didn't say this yesterday, but thank you for opening my eyes to Jack. He had me fooled." She patted the side of her bed for him to come over and have a seat beside her, and he sat down on the edge of the bed. "I love you," she said in a loving voice that made him love her more, if that was even possible.

"You are welcome, but it wasn't necessary, it goes without saying."

He leaned into her to plant one of those hot, sweet kisses that ignited the fires deep within him. He broke away to look at her, and he wanted so badly to tell her about his past, but he was still nervous. He knew that she loved him but was not sure if she would still understand his lie.

She looked long and hard at him before she asked, "Do you have any plans for New Year's Eve?"

"Not a thing, but I was kind of hoping that we would share it together!" He was subtly hinting that he was really counting on spending it with her.

"How would you like to join me and the rest of the family at a party with Larry and Lonnie?" she said, not really thinking that she needed to explain or put in their last names, assuming that he would automatically know who she was talking about.

"As in Krump?" He sounded totally awed, not forgetting that this was the world she traveled in. How could he ask her to join him in his simple life? He wanted to marry her. He knew that she was the woman for him, but was he the right man for her? She was used to the glamour life, mixing amongst the rich and famous, and he was just a cowboy.

"Rick, is something wrong?" She looked at him with a watchful stare. He looked like he had just lost his best friend. Like despair had taken over his heart.

"It's nothing, really. I am just so happy that we have finally taken this next step and stopped the games. I don't want to ever hurt you. It's important to me that you know that."

Still, he didn't look quite right to Amy. Something deeper was troubling him. She knew better than to probe. When he was ready she was sure that he would tell her.

She paused to ask the next question. She had to truly know how he felt about her posing nude. "How do you feel about your girlfriend posing for a smut magazine?"

He surprised her just a little with his response. "*Proud!* It doesn't matter to me, because I love you and trust you completely to do the right thing for you."

Amy invited him into her bed. This time, he would undress her, admiring her beauty, taking it all in. It still bothered him about being in the witness protection program and that he hadn't come clean in telling her, and their little bit of lifestyle difference, but he was confident that they could overcome these obstacles. His contact at the FBI hadn't called him back yet. He needed to talk to them, to find out what information he could tell her.

He would think about what kind of life they would share later. Right now his body was telling him to shut up and pay attention to the growing desire that he felt for this amazing woman. He caressed every inch of her body, photographing it to his memory as he slowly, seductively undressed her.

She laid there in admiration as her own desires were welling up inside her. He blew softly across her taut nipples, sending shivers of pleasure through her body. He was taking his time exploring every inch of her magnificent, firm-in-all-the-right-places body. He slid down her as he approached her womanhood. Her warm, sensuous, sweet-smelling mound. His fingers found their way amongst her trimmed auburn curls, and he toyed with her swelling clit. She moaned, she squirmed under his touches, and he pressed his nose closer. His tongue took a short swipe…Yum, tasty, sweet. Another lick, longer, more as he continued to rub her clit. He inserted one finger, two, and three…She was moaning and squirming with the thrusts of his fingers, calling out his name. He believed on his first touch that he found her G-spot.

If this is just what his fingers can do to me, I can't wait for the real thing, to have his cock thrusting and pounding inside of me. How much longer is he going to make me wait? I need to tell him now, before…"Oh, my Goddddd…Yes, oh, sweet yes," she huskily pronounced, one orgasm down as she bucked beneath him and tightened her muscles around his fingers. Several more to come, she hoped! A series of yeses in between, finger thrusts, and more groans of pure pleasure were telling him that she was very close to another orgasm, and then, without another word, her thighs tightened again and she let go.

"Why don't you, umm…come up here?"

He quickly obeyed her command, and his tongue probed her mouth to find hers waiting eagerly to dance with his. They shared hot, sensual kisses, his hands roaming her body again. She broke from the kiss. "Someone is wearing too much clothing."

He quickly undressed himself, not wanting to stop pleasing her as it was giving him so much pleasure…Before he could get back on the bed, she sat up to the edge of the bed. Staring back at her was his cock. She had never had oral sex before, but what he just did to her was awesome, and now it was her turn to give some of that pleasurable feeling back.

She reached out and placed one hand around his enormous erection and the other cupped his balls, and she gently started to rub them. She started to stroke his erection, sliding her hand up and down. She watched his face, and he quivered as she leaned forward and her tongue licked its way around him like an ice cream cone. Then, in one quick swoop, she engulfed his cock into her mouth, suckling up and down, making slurping noises and moans as his hands found their way to the back of her head, helping her motion, not quite sure how far she was willing to take it.

He thought it was only fair to warn her of his impending release. “Ummm, Ames.” There were slurps and lip-smacking actions as she lifted her eyes to listen to him. “Hon, I’m about to explode…” She continued, ignoring his comment. “Oh, sweet Jesus…yes, oh, yes.” As he helped her, he thrust forward, sending his cock deeper into her mouth. It happened, her first oral orgasm. He came. He was still coming. She licked her lips, surprised at its sweet yet slightly salty flavour. Its texture was sticky.

Still watching him, she took what was on her hands and rubbed her crotch. “Baby, you turn me on fire…” He pushed her back on the bed and parted her legs wider. He fell into position, not wanting to waste any more time. She helped guide his cock into her, not that he needed any guidance. She just couldn’t wait any longer. He pumped, in and out, slow thrusts, hips moving in circular motions, her rhythm in tune with his. The pumping action quickened. Thrusting harder, trying to get deeper, he couldn’t get close enough to her. His balls smacked up against her. She raised her ass into the air a little more, and he held her there, a few more thrusts…In unison, they said, “Oh, yes…” He rolled over to half sit and half lie on the side of the bed and turned to look at her, waiting for another response. None was really needed.

The sound of little feet in the hallway told them that time had flown by, that Andrew was awake and soon everyone else would be, too, that it was time to get up and enjoy this fabulous day, their first Christmas together, with plenty more to come.

They both flopped back down on the bed, and he rolled over to her, enjoying the view.

“I’m so in love with you. I don’t know how or when I realized it,” she said, looking into his sedate eyes that told her everything that she already knew. He loved her. “I don’t know what I will do with my time once the photo shoot is through. There is a good possibility that

Vidal Sassoon will fire me once they find out about the pictures. I thought that it wouldn't matter to me, but I think that I was just trying to be brave and prepare myself for the worse that could very well happen. This has been my life for quite some time, yet part of me doesn't want to leave you, either," she continued. He wasn't saying a word yet, just lying and staring at her.

"I don't want you to give up anything for me, I will adjust. I won't lie and say that I won't miss you when you go to New York, London, Paris, or wherever they send you, 'cause I will like crazy. But I have the ranch here to keep me otherwise occupied." Taking her hand into his and looking at her, he continued. "Ames, I have complete and utter faith in our love, that nothing will shake it, and if they decide that they want you to keep modeling after this next shoot, then so be it."

"How did I get so lucky? I have done it all. Out with a bang! You have just made this so much easier for me. It is time for this model to step aside, while things are still good to her." She leaned over and planted a big, sloppy kiss on his lips.

Chapter Eleven

They watched as snow fell to make it a white Christmas. They spent Christmas morning gathered around the tree in the family room watching Andrew play with his new toys. She gave Philip his new briefcase, which he went nuts over and said was too expensive but graciously accepted. Sandra loved the new, special scarf from Milan. She even brought down Daddy's Stetson to give to Rick for Christmas. She talked it over with Sandra and she was fine with it. Hats were not Philip's thing, and she agreed that Rick should have it. He was ecstatic over the gift. It would be one of the most treasured items that he owned. He felt honoured to have been given their father's hat. She also gave him, upstairs, the pictures that Jack took, with a wink that told him that he could fantasize about her when they could not be together.

"Hey, there's still a couple of presents left under the tree!" Andrew scurried over to grab them, taking them to his dad to help him read the tags. "This one is for Aunt Amy, I can spell her name, it's easy, only three letters," his little, excited voice said as he carried the small box over to her. "Who's the other one for, Daddy?"

"It says it's for me!" He shook the long, narrow box. Everyone watched as he unwrapped it. Amy knew what it was. Sandi had told her earlier what she was going to do. It was a brown box. He lifted the lid, showing a quizzical expression on his face, and instantly he recognized the instrument inside to be a home pregnancy test stick. He took it out and looked at it more closely. Surprise overtook him. "Are we sure?" Although he had his suspicions, it was all he could muster…

"Yes, I saw the doctor two days ago. Everything is okay. We are going to have a baby in July," Sandi said as she excitedly walked over to Philip, who held out his arms to hug his adoring wife.

"A baby? Ewww, I don't want a baby," Andrew exclaimed, and everyone laughed.

"Andy, don't you want a brother or sister?" his father asked.

"Yeah, but a baby? They stink, and all they do is poop."

"Where did you hear that?" Sandi asked him as she lifted him into her arms.

"Molly's mom brought one home from the hospital, and she said that was all it did was poop and cry…"

"Awe, honey, I promise that this one won't do that, okay?" She hugged him.

"Okay, Mommy. Aunt Amy, what did you get?" His little body was squirming to get down now so that he could go back and play with his new toys more. He was losing interest in the baby talk.

She slowly unwrapped her gift. It was a jeweler's box. She looked at Rick for some kind of explanation. She continued, lifting the lid, and staring back at her was the most exquisite sapphire-and-diamond, marquise, three-stone-setting ring that she had ever laid eyes on…

"I'm speechless…I…" was all she could muster.

Philip cut in. "Better enjoy that one, Rick. It won't happen again. I can almost promise that," he chirped, laughing at Sandi as she swatted at his arm.

He walked over to her and got down on one knee. He took Amy's hand into his as he asked his next question in front of everyone that he knew mattered to her "Will you do me the honour of becoming my wife? Will you marry me?" He watched her go gaga over it.

She was in total shock. This was the last thing that she had expected. She knew that she loved him, but was she ready for marriage again? "Yes…" came out before her brain had a chance to register and reject him. "How long have you been planning this? When did you know?" she asked as she watched him get up and then planted a big kiss on his lips, leaving him wanting more. He took her left hand and placed the ring on her ring finger, his touch lingering.

"Yuk…get a room!" young Andrew proclaimed.

"Andrew!"

"I honestly don't know where he picked that up. I'm sorry, guys," Sandra said as she shook her head, coming over to examine the ring. Everyone was now laughing at Andrew's comment. Again, Sandra knew about Rick's intentions, he had run them by her the night before, and they both knew that it was just a matter of time before Amy saw the light and stopped fighting him.

"So many questions. It's my mother's. I've had it for some time now. I was just waiting for the right moment. I have known since the first time that I saw you that you were special," he told everyone in the room, looking adoringly at his new fiancée.

"How about some breakfast? I can have pancakes ready in no time! Who wants?" Sandi asked, trying to break the silence that filled the room and give them some alone time. It was something that they apparently needed and would get little of living in this house.

"I do, I do…" piped in little Andrew.

"Me, too." Philip came along.

Amy and Rick were still looking at each other. "Okay, lovebirds…break it up. This is a PG home," Sandra laughingly called behind her as she walked toward the kitchen to prepare breakfast.

They enjoyed a traditional pancake breakfast, eating in the kitchen rather than the formal dining room.

The rest of the day went kind of in slow motion as they just lazed around the house and ate way too much good food. Amy and Sandra were preparing a fabulous Christmas turkey dinner as the men talked in the family room, watching Andrew play with his toys.

Watching them from the kitchen, Amy asked Sandi, "So is this what a good marriage looks like?"

Turning to look at her, she said, "What do you mean? Philip and I have a good marriage, and you will, too, with Rick. Don't get me wrong, Ames. It takes a lot of hard work, but it is all worth it." Rubbing her not-yet-swollen belly, she smiled, as she was so happy about her condition.

"I'm just a little scared. I mean, I know and trust my love for Rick, but my lifestyle is so not what he has bargained for. Let's say that I do give it all up. I've been in the spotlight for so long the paparazzi will still follow my life. Is that really fair to Rick?" She loved Rick, there was no question in that, but she also didn't want to hurt him, and her failed marriage was partially to blame on the paparazzi…

"Ames, Rick loves you. He is well aware of your lifestyle! He is willing to take on that. He wants to make you happy and will do anything to follow that through. We have had our little talks. I have filled him in on what your life has been like. Perhaps the easiest way to solve the paparazzi issue is to make a formal interview, announce your wedding—your plans to keep it a quiet ceremony…" Amy turned to her sister to listen to her theory. Unfortunately she didn't really know how the paparazzi worked.

"Sandi, you have great intentions, but paparazzi don't work that way. Look at what they did to Lady Di and Prince Charles. They practically destroyed their lives. But you do have some good ideas."

On Boxing Day, Jack sent his contact at *Penthouse* the pictures that he just happened to have doubles of that he agreed to give them, along with a forged document allowing their release. She left him no alternative. He was in too deep to these guys. Gambling was as addictive as sex was with Amy. He was going to miss those soft, firm thighs rubbing against his.

A couple of days later, Sophie had called to tell her that all the editors that they had discussed had taken the bait and wanted the elusive Miss Amy Gordon as their Miss February centerfold, but one had indicated that they already had nudes of Amy and were not interested. Sophie made it clear that those had been obtained illegally and a lawsuit would be filed if they found their way into publication.

They backed off. And then they had to push the commercial for Vidal Sassoon back a couple of weeks, and Sassoon was good with that. Sophie explained to VS that Amy was going to do a spread for *Rustler* and they were okay with that, which was a great surprise to Amy. She was not going to have to give up her dreams just yet.

Amy found Rick hard at work down in the stables. She had to tell him the good news and that she decided to go back to New York and stay until after the photo shoot, which was to start the first week into the New Year, to finish packing up her apartment. She wanted to know if he wanted to join her. After some hemming and hawing about the work that he had here, he agreed to go and asked Felix to look after things for him. He explained to her that this was the time of year that they had to get their broodmares ready for breeding. He explained that they had to have them in the teasers, and ready for the first of the year if they expected any foals next year. She wanted him to be at the photo shoot with her for moral support and to ease his mind of what they were doing. She only assumed that the shoot would be at the studio of *Rustler*.

The drive back to New York was quiet, but not for lack of conversation. They both knew that words were not always necessary, that they just enjoyed each other's company, but if it had to be told, he was not one hundred percent comfortable being in the Big Apple. New York was never his place. He was a country boy at heart, and he was a bit nervous. His contact at the FBI told him to just be careful and try to stay out of the media, but this was what made her happy. He only hoped that he would not embarrass her at the Krump party on New Year's Eve.

She interrupted his thoughts, "Oh, I forgot to tell you that Larry called earlier. He has an interested buyer for the condo."

He glanced over at her, still trying to wrap his brain around these big names. *Who would have ever guessed that I, Richard Durham, would ever be rubbing elbows with the elite Mr. Larry Krump, and who knows who else?* Was he really ready for this kind of life? Yes, he would do anything for her. He focused his attention back to the road, saying, "That is wonderful news, sweetie. But if we sell the penthouse, where would we stay when we come to New York when you have to work?" He focused on the road but glanced at her out of the corner of his eyes.

"I have been giving that a lot of thought, too. I still have to talk to Sophie, but I believe that you should be the first to know…" She paused to see if she got a reaction from him. "I am going to give this all up! After the assignment in Hawaii in March, that will be it. I'm not sure what is in the cards next, as far as my career." She laid it all out for him. This was not where she intended to tell him about her decision, placing her hands in her lap and twiddling her thumbs nervously, still waiting for a reaction.

"It's a good thing that this new car has a navigation system to help me find your apartment," was all she got out of him! She was stunned. She just told him that she was giving all this up.

Pulling up in front of her building, put the car into park for the attendant, and he got out and went around to open her door, helping her out.

"I didn't reply to your comment, as I think that it deserves a much more in-depth discussion, which we can conclude once upstairs." He held her hand as they walked into the building, feeling her smiling glare at him.

Chapter Twelve

Once inside the lobby, she introduced Rick to Markus, the front doorman, and told him that they would be staying for a couple of days and that Rick was to come and go as he wished. They rode the elevator in silence in anticipation of what awaited them upstairs. Christmas Day was the first and only time so far that they had ever made love, and it was one of the most beautiful experiences that she had ever had. She knew that this burning desire that was building up was going to come to a head, and with no interruptions it was going to happen here. Maybe tonight? But first things first, he indicated that they needed to discuss her decision to leave her modeling career behind once they started their new life together.

She showed him around the apartment and told him to make himself comfortable, that for as long as they owned it to consider it his home. They came to a stop at the master suite. In the doorway, he pulled her into his arms and held her there before he started to place soft, light kisses on her forehead, over her nose, down her cheeks, and finally on her lips, her soft, subtle lips that tasted like strawberry wine. He probed her mouth with his tongue, which began to dance around once granted permission. Hands started to fly, and who knew whose were doing what by just looking, but their clothes ended up on the floor, and they were both totally naked! With enough light, he was taking in every inch of his beautiful goddess. He stepped back just briefly before he took her up into his arms to carry her over to the bed to carefully examine his winning trophy.

"Open your eyes, Amy…I want you to watch me as we make love," he said to her as he climbed onto the bed and laid on his side beside her so that he could lay more kisses and caresses along her flawless body, arouse her desires, and send her to ecstasy and back. He watched her watching him as he cupped her breast into his hand as she let out soft moans, and her breathing was electrifying. He took her already-erect nipple between his forefinger and thumb and rubbed gently, keeping it taut, sending her further into their world of pleasure and beyond. He slowly kissed her stomach, planting more kisses as he reached her soft bed of curls at her mound, and then he slipped his hand between her legs, placing, ever so lightly, touches against her thighs, making her squirm under his touch.

"Rick…It has to be now. I can't wait. It will happen without you if you don't…" She felt his rather large erection probing her thigh. He had climbed on top of her, the tip of his cock just grazing the edge of her feminine folds, just before he plunged into her. Lifting her legs up over his arms to give him a better angle, he felt her thrusting action come into a rhythm with his, slowly at first. Then the passion and desire took over her moaning and raspy tones as she called out his name and told him that she was very close to orgasm, and he wanted to come and release his own at the same time.

"Harder, harder, yes, yes, oh, God yes."

He pumped a little harder as she instructed. One final thrust, and he felt the wetness surround him. They both came at the same time. He collapsed on top of her. He rolled over, breathing heavily with sweat dripping down his forehead, and she gently wiped it away from his brow.

"That is the best lovemaking that I have ever experienced." They both said it in unison, and laughter broke out between them. "Better than Christmas?" he questioned lovingly, knowing that there was no response needed for that one.

Amy got off the bed and reached for her robe, turning to look at this dapper male lying on her bed and feeling like she was the luckiest woman on the planet. Hands on her hips, head cocked to one side, she said, "So, we need to discuss my leaving the business? What happened to supporting whatever decision that I make?"

He gave his head a quick shake. What was she doing? They just had explicit sex, it was mind-blowing, and now of all times, she chose to discuss this? He gave a look that just said all that…

"Come back here. We can talk about that later. I want to make love to you all night long, make you hurt to walk from all the things that I want to do to you…" Lovingly, he patted the bed, trying to get her to come back to their love nest.

She just stood there glaring at him, trying not to be sexy. She didn't want to let it wait to fester and become something more. "Don't give me that sexy look, mister. I don't want this to be blown out of proportion." She scampered back over to the bed, jumping in beside him.

"Okay, okay…Let's talk about it." He paused to let her start her argument so that he could counteroffer his reason for not letting her quit her career.

"All right then, thank you. I am ready to take the next step in my life, and that is to be by your side. I have had enough of the limelight. I'm ready. And before you say that you don't want me to do this because of you, I'm not. Even if I hadn't already been in love with you and this mess had come out, I still would have gone through with this photo shoot. I am tired, I am getting older, and the camera adds pounds and years to us. I want to go out looking my best, and I truly believe that this is it. There, I have said my piece, and I am sorry if you don't agree with my decision. It will have to be something that we both live with or find another way to work it out."

"Oh, baby…I'm so sorry. I don't want us to fight. I *will* support your decision, if you are sure that this is what you want! I love you, and I am sorry that I made fun or light of the situation. That was not my intention. I only want you to be happy, and I can only hope that I help make that happen." Taking her into his arms, caressing her back, feeling her little sobs, he held her back to look into her face. He wiped away the tear that slid down her cheek. "Honey, don't cry. It will be okay…That I promise with my whole being." He embraced her again.

"Rick, that is the sweetest thing that anyone has ever done for me. I have faith that we can accomplish anything together." She lifted her head to give him a kiss.

They had dinner out that night, and the paparazzi followed once they saw her getting into the cab. She talked with him and asked how he felt about the invasion. "Honestly, I think that it is something that we really do need to talk about back at the apartment, but for tonight, let's just enjoy our dinner and leave it at that." Their dinner was quiet and enjoyable, their first date. They discussed a date for the wedding. She was thinking about June. She always wanted a June wedding. They both agreed that it should be at the ranch and something small with a few intimate friends and family.

"You have not really told me anything about yourself. Do you have any siblings? Where did you grow up? Things that a wife should know." They were sitting at the table, lounging over wine.

"Well…Let's see, I was born in Calgary, Alberta, my parents are Alison and Ashton Durham. I have two older brothers and a younger sister. I graduated from U of Calgary with a bachelor of science with a further study in equestrian breeding of thoroughbreds. It was not my parent's first choice for me, but I have loved horses my whole life." He took her hand into his. "Now you tell me something that I don't already know about you."

He quickly had to change the topic from him. He needed desperately tell her the truth…everything, but not here.

"My life has been pretty much an open book, but what hasn't become public knowledge they make up. I'm twenty-five, born to Ivan and Kassandra Gordon. I have an identical twin that is mere minutes older than I. My birthday is February…"

"Would you like anything else tonight, sir?" the waiter interrupted her politely.

"No, I think that will be everything. The check will be fine. Thank you," he replied. "And where were we? Oh yes, your birthday? Is there anything else that I don't know about you?" he asked with a sparkle in his eyes.

"February 14. I don't know what you have read about me, so I really don't know what I can tell you. Oh, I know, this was never made public knowledge…" Removing her hand from his, she gave a wave over her breasts. "These are not my real boobs! Bet you never guessed that one." She laughed.

Shock overtook his expression. "Okay, you managed to make me speechless…No, I would not have guessed that. They of course feel and look fabulous. Guess the question would be why?"

"Bet that doesn't happen too often either…Speechless, I mean. Thanks, why?" She continued to hold his hand. She waited to continue, as the waiter brought them their check. Before he left, Rick took out his wallet and handed him his Visa card. The waiter disappeared again.

"I think that the rest of this conversation is best for the privacy of our place," he said as the waiter returned for his signature. He picked up her coat and helped her put it on. They hailed a cab and returned home for the remainder of the evening.

In the comfort of their living room, they continued their conversation from the restaurant. She confessed her reason for getting her implants. Feeling a bit insecure in just how sexy her body really was, she felt that her boobs were not big enough, so she had them enlarged from an A cup to a generous B cup. He revealed his birthday was September 24.

"Ames…I need to tell you something, and please don't interrupt…It's really important for me to tell you this…I've tried a couple of times but have failed with the courage that I need, but I find that it can't wait any longer." He paused for a couple of seconds as he gathered both the courage and the right words to tell her. "My real name is Craig Andrews…Before you interrupt…My family is in witness protection. My father put Philadelphia's crime lord Sontiago away almost twenty years ago." He was stumbling, and she could hear the tremor in his voice as he continued. "Most of everything that I have told you is the truth. My parents' real names are Patricia and Eric Andrews, my father did pass away a couple of years ago, everything else is true." He now waited for the other proverbial shoe to drop.

"Can I speak now? Are you done?" she asked, looking into his very distraught, caring eyes with a softness of her own that told him that she was not upset, that she cared.

"Yes…are you mad at me?" He anxiously waited for her to answer and tell him that everything would be okay.

"Well, that is quite a mouthful! I believe you, if that concerns you. I am not sure why you decided to tell me! Isn't that breaking some kind of rule? The last thing that I want is to put you or your family into danger." She felt the need to embrace him and let him feel that she was okay with what he just told her. She moved closer to him on the couch and did just that, running her hands up and down his back, patting his shoulder. "We will work this out. I love you, Rick…Um, what do I call you?" she asked, a little teasing in her tone.

"I talked to the FBI agent looking after our case. He seems to think that since my father is dead, they will leave us alone, but I should still try to stay out of the media," he said, still holding her and enjoying the comfort in knowing that this did not matter to her, that she understood the small lie of omission. "Do you think that we can do that? I want the world to know that you are mine, but I really don't want my picture plastered in the papers or have people know that I am in the WPP, either! You can call me anything that your beautiful heart desires…but to keep the ruse up, I think that in public it should still be Rick. I will marry you as Craig Andrews! I want our life to be real and not a lie."

"I understand, and we'll work this all out. To the world, no matter what my married name becomes I will always be known as Amy

Gordon. I will have to come up with something to tell Sophie. We need her help to keep it private."

They agreed that they would have to share some of this with Sophie and her family, and that was it.

All in all, it was a very enjoyable evening. It was something that she had not had in such a long time. It felt genuine and real. Since they agreed on a wedding date, she thought that she better call and enlighten Sandra and Sophie. It was still early, and he was watching a hockey game on TV, so she took advantage of that and made her calls. Sandra first…

"Hi, Anna, is Sandi there, please? It's Amy." She waited as Anna got Sandra to the phone.

"Amy…What's up? I am getting excited about the party. Philip gave me his platinum card and let me go shopping in the city. Can you believe that?" Her sister sounded so excited that she was having a hard time getting a word in edgewise…*Oh, wait, a silent breath.* She jumped in. "We have set a date!"

"What? I mean, when?"

"We decided on June 20. I always wanted a June wedding," she announced.

"Cool. That is awesome. I will mark our calendar. That gives us some time to get the invitations out. How many guests are we talking about? We are having it here, right?" She still sounded excited, this time for her sister.

"Yes, we plan to have it at the ranch. We are going to keep it simple, family and a few intimate friends," she replied to her sister.

"We will talk more about this in a couple of days when Philip and I get there." With that, they chatted a little longer before saying good night.

The next few days flew by. They had spent time doing some sightseeing. She wanted to introduce him to all her friends and to the finer things that she enjoyed, like the Statue of Liberty and the Empire State Building, just to name a few places.

They met with Larry to go over the selling contract, and he didn't lead her astray. He did just as he promised, got her the absolute best price for her suite. She stood to make a substantial profit over her original purchase price. The seven-figure number stunned Rick. He had no idea that an apartment in New York held that kind of value. They talked about what to do with it all. She was insistent that they put it into the ranch, to make his dreams and her daddy's dreams come true, putting them on the race circuit. She wasn't sure just how to do that but had faith that he would.

She left him at the apartment to manage the packers coming in to pack up the last of her stuff as she went to her meeting with Sophie to discuss the details with *Rustler* and her leaving the business after the Hawaii assignment.

"Amy, darling…I can't believe that you want to quit the business. I am still getting all kinds of offers. People still want you."

"But will they still want me after the *Rustler* photos hit the stand? That is my big question. I don't want to become a 'has-been.' I want different things in my life now, and that includes Rick and whatever life we can create for ourselves. I am sorry, Sophie, but my decision is final. I thank you from the bottom of my heart for everything that you have ever done for me. You have gone over and beyond the call of duty. You are one of my dearest friends." Her hands were trembling as she let out little sobs. These were life-altering changes she was making.

"Okay, you win for now, but don't blame me if I come back from time to time with offers. I strongly believe that they will continue to pour in. You didn't get here by luck. You worked your ass off, and it shows. People respect you and will continue to do so." She paused to take a sip of her Swiss mocha. "By the way, *Rustler* wants to do the photo shoot at the ranch, in the stables."

"Is this negotiable? I mean, it's not just my home, it's a family home. I have to discuss it with Sandi and Philip."

"I am not sure, we never put too much discussion on that detail. Everything is negotiable, darling."

"All right, I've got to go. Sandi and Philip are due in this afternoon. Oh yeah, before I forget. Rick proposed and I accepted. We have set the date for June 20." She pretended to rise from her chair to leave.

"Wait just a minute, darling. You can't just spring something as important as that you are getting married and walk away. Are we going to publicize this tidbit of info? If so, how much do you want the public to know?"

She sat back down…She had to let Sophie know. "Wait a minute there, Soph. We can't do a big release. I mean, no photos please. I am about to tell you something here that *must* be kept confidential." She fell silent for a moment before she continued "…So you see, his whole family is in the witness protection program, and I will not risk his life for my own benefit."

They discussed it and decided to wait until after the New Year and that it would be a simple release, with only her at the release, explaining that her fiancé had work to do at the ranch.

A few minutes later, she rose again to leave.

"Okay, discuss it with them and let me know ASAP. We are up against the wire for deadlines," Sophie said as she, too, rose and walked over to the door and gave her friend a hug with a kiss on each cheek.

Chapter Thirteen

Sandra and Philip were already at the apartment when she returned home from her meeting with Sophie. She welcomed them to her pad. She gave Sandra the grand tour before going to get ready for the party that night. It had been a couple of days since she saw her and Amy was a little concerned for her condition, given the fact that she'd had previous miscarriages in the past. "Sandi, are you okay? You look a little pale. We can cancel tonight if you want?"

"Miss the opportunity…of meeting 'the' Larry Krump and his wife…Lonnie! Not a chance in hell, sista! I will be fine. It's just a little indigestion from dinner. It will pass." The ladies parted into separate rooms to get ready.

"It's almost time to leave, Ames! Are you guys ready yet? Larry is going to wonder what on earth has happened to you if we show up late!" He was getting anxious and nervous at the same time. These were Amy's friends and he wanted to make a good impression.

"I'm coming, and don't you worry, Larry will be more surprised if I show up on time rather than late, I'm almost always late for his parties," she retorted with a hint of laughter following. She came out of the bedroom wearing a sleek, mint-green, strapless number that hugged every curve she had and showed just enough cleavage. His expression said it all to her. Amy told him that he needed to pick up his jaw when they reached the lobby. They all laughed. Sandi and Philip were ready to go. Amy had rented a limo for this evening so that no one had to worry about drinking and driving.

They arrived at Larry and Lonnie's place in record time. The paparazzi were outside, as expected. It was the scene for New Year's Eve, and anyone that knew anyone had been invited.

In the car, Amy advised anyone that didn't want their face plastered on the paper the next day to just hold up their hand to cover their face, that the paparazzi were usually pretty good and accepted that.

They snapped a few photos of the girls as they got out of the limo and asked for a photo of Amy and her date…She corrected them and at the same time asked them not to take their picture, that there was a press conference in a couple of days and they could take all the pictures that they wanted then. Then she announced to the world, "Not my date, he is my fiancé, his name is Richard Durham…" They agreed and respected her wish for no photos that night. As she looked into his face, searching for his reaction, he smiled proudly and politely at them. He wasn't totally comfortable. He had to remind himself that this was her world, and if he wanted to be a part of it, this came with it.

They walked inside and were greeted by their host and hostess. Amy introduced her family.

The food and drinks were plenty and the music was great as usual. They mingled. They danced and mingled some more. She could not believe that this was her world. She was feeling all the phony vibes in the room for the first time since she had been attending these parties. Perhaps it was the fact that she had found her roots, going back home. For the first time since she had mentioned giving up modeling, it felt right. Most of these people were not her real friends, they were just acquaintances that she met along her career path. Of all the people there that night, Amy could honestly say that the only ones that she would trust were Larry and Lonnie. But they were also the ones that she spent most of her time with, as she and Lonnie went back to when she first started modeling.

It was getting late, and she was getting tired. Emotionally she had been a busy woman for one day. Besides, she would rather be back at their place celebrating the New Year alone with him. She was never really into these parties to begin with. She had a lot to be thankful for and never took any of this for granted. She enjoyed her work but was looking forward to a more relaxed lifestyle. In her heart she knew that she was making the right decision. Rick convinced her to stay just a little longer. He was enjoying himself, and so were Sandra and Philip. It wasn't every day that they got to mingle with this crowd and meet celebrities like Joan Rivers, Geraldo, Billy Ray Cyrus, and Regis Philbin, just to name a few. She reluctantly agreed, seeing the fascination and excitement on his face.

She told Larry and Lonnie about their engagement, and much to her surprise, Larry made a formal announcement to all their friends. All in all they had a great time.

Everyone cheered, bringing in the New Year and a new life filled with happiness and love at the sound of the ball dropping.

He kissed his fiancée, and it didn't bother him who saw them. It was with passion that had promises for what waited for them when they returned home.

They stayed a little longer to thank everyone for their congratulations and well wishes. A few asked what their plans were for the future. Their replies were that they didn't know, but it was going to be a good life wherever they ended up.

* * * *

Sandra and Philip decided to stay on a few more days after Amy and Rick's persistent pleas. They told them that they wouldn't be intruding, since Amy had things to get ready for with the photo shoot happening next week. The only other thing left was to discuss the location with the others. They were sitting down to breakfast the morning after the party when she looked around the kitchen, trying to figure out how to approach the topic. They really hadn't talked about it since she mentioned that she was doing it.

"I have a favour to ask…" She jumped in with all fours. "*Rustler* wants the location to be at the ranch." There, she said it. It was out there. She wasn't sure how everyone felt about it.

"What? Ames, it's one thing to be doing this, but at the ranch?" Rick was the first one to comment.

"What are the ramifications if we don't all agree?" Sandra piped in. Philip sat there in silence.

"Sophie hasn't gotten back to me yet on that. They haven't said that it was negotiable or not. I trust *Rustler*'s editor and photographer to do this with taste…" She hadn't told them yet that she wouldn't be completely nude, like she originally thought. It wasn't going to be as bad as she thought.

"What about the ranch's reputation? We're a horse breeder," Rick jumped in again. He wasn't sure that he wanted the ranch hands watching as his future wife was photographed in the nude. It was one thing for them to buy the smut, he couldn't stop that, and that really didn't bother him, as he continued to say. He interrupted her thoughts.

Watching his reaction, she thought that she had him pegged. It wasn't so much the location as it was who was going to be there. "Sweetie, it's going to be a closed set, no matter where the final shoot is going to be. No one will be allowed on that is not authorized by me that doesn't need to be there." Seeing a sigh of relief consume him, she knew that she hit the nail on the head.

"All right, all right, I give in…" he said, throwing his hands up in the air, as if he was really fighting her on this. Sandra and Philip also agreed to allow Mystical to be used. She would call Sophie at home later to let her know.

The next few days were blessed and full of fun. She was getting a little worried about Sandra. She had noticed that she was still having morning sickness. She questioned her on it. Sandra said that she had visited the walk-in clinic yesterday and they assured her that everything was okay, that the baby's heartbeat was strong, that it would pass.

As a special gift to Sandra and Philip, she gave them tickets to "Annie Get Your Gun" starring Reba McEntire, with special backstage passes. Reba was Sandi's favourite singer, and she was ecstatic about the night out. She told her that she could choose whatever she wanted from her closet to wear, that it wouldn't be much longer that she could borrow her clothes. She teasingly laughed as she said it.

Amy and Rick were staying in tonight, watching TV. She had been feeling tired and a little queasy. Too much excitement in such a short span of time is what she thought. He made her some hot green tea to help settle her tummy and rubbed her back. They went to bed early. Lying there just holding each other was all they needed tonight. Neither of them heard when Sandra and Philip arrived back at the apartment after their fabulous night out on the town.

Sandra and Philip were quiet when they returned. Not giving it another thought, they shared the bathroom at home, but something was different tonight. She was different, beautiful. He was half-undressed when she asked him to help with the zipper at the back, and he obliged. Grasping the zipper between his thumb and middle finger, he let his forefinger caress the inside of the dress as he slid the zipper down. Slowly he lifted each strap and slid them down off her sensuous shoulders, letting her dress fall to the floor. He reached for the bra clasp at the back, letting it fall to the floor, and she just stood there, watching them in the mirror. He undid his own pants and stepped out of them.

She gasped with excitement when she saw his erection. He was butt naked behind her, and he placed sweet, light kisses along her neck as his hands ran up and down her arms, sending sparks through her body. This was mind-blowing. They never did this at home. He placed his hand on her abdomen then gently twirled her around to face him before he picked her up and placed her on the bathroom counter. She grabbed her panties as he frantically pulled them down. Leaning in, he took her swollen nipple into his mouth and hungrily suckled on it, placing his other hand on her hot, wet mound, fingers mingling amongst her moist curls, caressing her folds, finding her entrance.

She threw her head back as she let out soft little moans, trying to be careful that no one could hear what they were doing there. She grabbed her other tit and started to squeeze and play with her nipple. He found what he was looking for, picking her up and wrapping her legs around his waist. His cock slid into her opening. He carried her over to the door and braced them as he let out groans of pleasure, pumping, thrusting, in, out, back and forth, making circling motions with his hips, her rhythm in sync. Her arms tightened around his neck as she placed kisses along his shoulders. He was about to explode inside his wife. With the last thrust, she let out a shrill cry of pleasure. He felt her climax and an explosion took place, still holding her. He placed a few more kisses along her neck.

"Baby, you were awesome. We have to remember this position when we get home," he huskily said to her as he slid out and put her down on her feet.

"I know. You were awesome yourself. I can't believe that we did this, especially here, in my sister's bathroom, with her across the hall." Both let out a soft laugh, gathered their clothes, and sneaked down the hall to their room. Where they laid in bed and talked some more before falling asleep.

Chapter Fourteen

It was Sandra and Philip's last night in New York. She took them out for dinner to the Affinia Dumont Hotel over on East Thirty-Fourth Street. It wasn't going to be every day that she could spoil her family with elegant dinners. They ate and talked for hours, had a fabulous time, and Sandra was astonished as she watched the celebrities come and go in the restaurant. This was a fantastic minivacation. She was having the time of her life, just a little green with envy over the lifestyle that her sister lived, but she wouldn't trade in hers with Philip, Andrew, and now their latest addition coming into their family.

The next morning, the sisters gave each other kisses with "see ya really soon" hugs good-bye. Amy had an appointment this afternoon with *Rustler*'s editor, Michael, and Mitch, the photographer. She invited Rick to join her so that he knew exactly what they were getting into and to give them her bio that they wanted to go with her photos. She provided them with all the information that they were looking for. The only thing that they thought would be best to leave out was the fact that she was getting married. Rick stepped up and said, "Absolutely not. She's going to be my wife. I am proud of her and her accomplishments and don't want others to think that she's available."

The editor, who in turn sat there with a smug look on his face, looked at Amy and asked, "And what is your opinion on this?"

Looking at Rick, she said, "I happen to agree with my fiancé. I think that it is important that your readers know the real me. And that includes the fact that I recently got engaged to this wonderful man." She reached for his hand as they sat side by side.

The rest of the meeting went really well. They discussed the location, Mystical Thoroughbred Breeding Ranch, using their stables, and advised that it was a closed set and that any employees should be made aware of this. Mitch stood up, lifting Amy by the arm, taking her over to the window to examine her. He lifted his arm and with a twirling motion asked her to turn around slowly. "Ummm, you look absolutely divine. We will have so much fun with this." He looked at Rick for his reaction, not getting what he had hoped for, the "jealous boyfriend" response. Instead Rick just sat there fuming under his own skin, thinking he was going to be able to handle this, but it was much harder than he originally thought. He did not like the idea of other men fondling his girl. He shot Amy a couple of glances that were telling her that he was getting uncomfortable. She tried to hurry the meeting along and help ease Rick's mind.

She asked Mitch, "So what are your plans and vision for this shoot?"

"I was thinking that, since you grew up around horses and we are doing the shoot at the ranch, we would have you first sitting on one, then a couple shots brushing the mane, and then a couple lounging on a bale of hay! How does that sound?"

"Prickly." She first laughed. "How much or little clothing will I be wearing?"

"Ha ha ha." Mitch came back with, "I thought maybe a little, skimpy two-piece bathing suit showing some of that marvelous cleavage that you own."

A look of surprise came across Rick's face, and he turned to look into Amy's eyes. "What…I thought that this was to be a nude scene?" Not having ever been interested in looking at smut magazines before, he really had no idea what was expected.

They all chuckled, and Michael explained, "Rick…We don't have to have nudes of every model that we put into our magazine, and since Amy here is the world's top fashion model, we want this in taste. Yes, we will show some skin, but she will be completely covered up, not revealing any intimate or private parts of her body. We just want to enhance her beauty. Give the readers something to fantasize about. I hope that this helps and gives you a different opinion of *Rustler* and what we want to accomplish."

A sigh of relief overcame Rick. This was a much better idea. This he could live with and accept. They continued to discuss the day for the shoot and what they needed to have set up. According to Mitch, Amy was such a professional and not one of her photographers had anything bad to say about her work or ethics. They ended on confirmation of meeting at Mystical Ranch that Wednesday afternoon to set up for Thursday and asked if the stable hands would be willing to give them a hand and control the horse. Rick confirmed that he was still the only one that would be on set and he could provide all the assistance that they would need. And Amy would send over the bio script proof tomorrow by courier.

Amy took Rick out for dinner again that night. They discussed his relief over how the shoot was being conducted, and he told her that he was proud of her and now he was actually looking forward to the shoot. They talked about their plans once they were back at the ranch, and how the teasing was going with Mystery.

As promised by *Rustler,* the bio arrived around 10:00 a.m. the next day. Amy opened the package and proof read the bio.

Name: Amy Louise Gordon

Age: 25

Bust: 38 Waist: 30 Hips: 37

Status: Single—but recently engaged to a hot thoroughbred breeder and ranch owner

Favourite food: Lasagna

Favourite drink: Water

Hair colour: Auburn

Eye colour: Hazel-green

Amy grew up in a small village north of Toronto, Ontario, Canada. Her father was none other than the well-respected Ivan Gordon, who was best known for breeding thoroughbreds. She has an identical twin sister. She is well known for her prestigious career as a fashion model, having traveled the world to exotic places like Paris, France, Milan, Italy, and Sydney, Australia, just to name a few. More recently Amy has become unavailable, as she has become engaged.

It went on to say that she enjoyed growing up with the horses and that she did not have a college or university degree of any kind, which was acceptable, and it was all the truth. They wanted to keep Rick's name out of the picture, they didn't want any unnecessary publicity on him. She agreed to what was printed and signed the release for publication and returned it by courier to the *Rustler* office.

The movers had finished packing up all her things from the condo and were having them put into storage. She took one last look around the place as a double-check that everything had been packed and to say good-bye. It was a little tearful, but she was ready to move onto the next phase of her life…Rick and the ranch.

The *Rustler* team arrived as agreed, and the stable was set up the way that Mitch had described it to them, including the heaters in the stables to help keep it warm for Amy and the others. Mitch kept to his promise, Amy was clothed in a tacky, two-piece bathing suit for one set of photos—sitting on the horse, they sprayed some water over her to look like she had just come from a swim, and she leaned into the mane of Fate. Then they had her change into this slinky, lace, olive-green bra and matching thong panties…That didn't impress him, these guys looking at her ass, his ass. These pictures were taken leaning against Fate, combing his mane, climbing up onto him, showing off Amy's firm buttocks. It went very well, and everyone was happy. Not as happy as Rick, as it was a twofold for him, to have the photo shoot done and his stables back to normal. They had work to do. He had horses to train and breed if they were going to have any new foals this fall.

Amy had Rick's clothes and other belongings moved into the main house, and they occupied the guest room until her room was finished being redecorated. They all agreed that Daddy and Momma's room would make an awesome nursery for the newest addition arriving this year to their family. The girls were not ready to go through their parents' belongings just yet, so they had them put into the attic so that when the time came they could.

January was a busy month for her. After her photo shoot with *Rustler,* she had to go back to New York the following week to do the commercial for the hair care company, who in turned agreed to put her up in a hotel suite at the Ritz-Carlton. She hated having to leave the ranch so soon, and that included Rick, but she understood that he could not just run away with her to every assignment she had, that he had to work, especially if they were to make this the best thoroughbred ranch on this side of the Great Lakes. They were starting small. Their dream was to be the best this side of the Atlantic.

This was something different for her. She had never done a commercial before, so it was exciting. The director and her assistant were absolutely fabulous, and they walked her through everything like how to say her lines. They had also hired someone to help teach her how to say them. There were a lot of similarities with photo shoots as shooting a commercial. There were the different angles for shooting, to get her best side, the face dusting to hide all the little imperfections. Again the cameraman was impressed with her work and the fact that they had little to touch up and they only had to do four takes. That was what impressed him the most. "You know, Amy, most of the models that I have had the opportunity of working with in commercials, they are so snotty and full of themselves that we have to spend almost two whole days doing takes, just to get them to cooperate. This has been a real pleasure working with you."

"Gee, thanks, Armon. I really appreciate that. I just look at it that we both have a job to do, and that the sooner that we can get it right the better that it is for everyone. Plus you made this really fun and easy to do. Thanks again."

They wrapped everything up by 4:30 p.m. Wednesday, which meant she could be back home by Thursday just after lunch. They had a little wrap party that night with the staff. Just a little thank-you for the wonderful job that everyone did. They wished her well and said that they would love to work with her again.

That took care of January, and February was turning out to be just as busy. She asked Sophie not to drum up any new business for her for the upcoming weeks. She had to have time to plan the wedding and she needed to be there for Sandra, as she was having a hard time with this pregnancy. And Sandra decided to give her law studies another chance.

She hired a crew to come in, and with Sandra's input they had the new nursery designed and painted. She decided not to remodel her old room since she and Rick had been talking about building a place on the west corner of the ranch.

Amy was enjoying this new phase of her life. She was beginning to think that giving up her career could prove to be a good thing. She could pamper her future husband's needs, actually learn the ropes of running a successful thoroughbred ranch, and learn how to train the best for racing. Since it was breeding season, Rick stayed late most nights down at the stables and he was the type of boss that worked right beside his employees. He would not ask them to do something that he himself would not do. She loved that about him as well. He was a very patient teacher. He helped her learn everything that she could about the ranch.

Sandra's birthday was today, February 13, since she was born at 11:55 p.m., and Amy was born at 12:05 a.m. on February 14. They threw her a small, intimate family party. Amy gave her a spa package that she could take any time that she wanted to. Philip and Andrew gave her this beautiful princess-cut amethyst ring. As he put the ring onto Sandra's finger, he told them the myth about the gem. "According to an old legend and general beliefs worldwide, this stone is considered to make the wearer calm and in control of various emotional levels."

"Do you really think that this will help with her mood swings, Philip?" Amy teasingly replied, smiling at her sister. She wasn't really looking for a comment back. She knew that Sandra was trying.

Later that night, Rick told her that he had a surprise for her tomorrow for her birthday and Valentine's Day. But she had to wait and could not pester him about it.

"About four o'clock, I would like for you to start getting ready. Pack a small overnight bag. We are going out for dinner and the night…no questions!" he said as he threw his Stetson onto the dresser and stripped before they climbed into bed.

"But how am I supposed to know what to wear? Should it be elegant, casual-formal, or just casual, as in jeans?" she asked as she rolled over on top of him, pinning down his arms so that he couldn't put them around her, as her face was mere inches from him, teasing and setting the mood.

"Let's go with casual—that little red dress in your closet should suffice. Now can I have my arms back? They are aching to touch you. It's been a long, lonely day." He pouted. And since he did it so well, she let go. Plus she had her own agenda. She, too, ached to have him touch her. She loved the way that she felt in his arms, so full of life, and he just energized her. They made love that was fun, playful, affectionate, intimate, and fulfilling before they fell asleep for the night, or was it the wee hours of the morning?

She woke the next morning surprised at the hour. She never slept this late in the morning, it was close to 10:30. She found a beautiful pink rose on his pillow with a note that read,

I will be thinking of you all day long. Anticipation rises when it's time to come up to the house after a hard day's work. You have brightened my life in so many ways. I don't know how I could ever thank you. I will try my absolute best to be the man that you need and want. Together I place my trust and love in us forever. Until tonight, I wait to have you all to myself. I love you with all my heart.

Love, Craig

Tears filled her eyes. She loved her little note and would treasure it always. She even noticed the name that he used. They had not discussed that since the night that he told her about his family and the reason behind his lie by omission. She lazily got out of bed to saunter down for some breakfast. She found an empty kitchen, and it appeared the whole house was empty.

She didn't really want to go to the stables and bug Rick today. She was so looking forward to tonight. As she got herself a bowl of Special K, she decided to go for a swim and do some laps, then use the workout room for some exercises. She had been feeling a little fat lately, not as firm as she liked to be. That should waste about three hours of her day. *What to do with last two and a half hours?*

It would only take her half an hour to get ready and packed to be waiting for him. Again she thought about the special evening that he had planned for them. He never mentioned anything about packing anything for him. Had he already packed his overnight bag? Hmmm, questions to ponder for the day. Before she really knew it, three o'clock came. Time to get ready for the *big* night. She so loved surprises, but it was still strange that she hadn't seen Sandra, Phillip, or even Andrew all day. She saw just about everyone else, and they wished her a happy birthday. She lingered in the shower, taking time to wash her hair and use the body soap that she knew drove Rick wild. Getting out, he startled her. She had not expected to see him standing there.

"Hi there. How was your day?" She walked over to him, carrying her towel to give him a kiss.

"I didn't want to bother you down in the stables today, so I stayed away." He had a sensual glaze in his eyes as he watched her adoringly and accepted her kiss. She tried to just give a little peck, but he pulled her in close to him, his mouth demanding attention from her lips. He still could not get enough of this woman. She simply drove him nuts. She broke their kiss first. "That was sweet. I love you, too. The rose and note this morning was a really nice touch," she said as she backed away from him to finish drying off and get ready.

"Happy birthday! It was a hectic day down there. Felix was mouthing off about something. I had to turn a deaf ear to deal with him later. I better jump into the shower. You can join me if you like…On second thoughts, no, stay out. I am quite sure that if you join me, we would get detained here. And dinner reservations are for five thirty," he said as he started to strip, and he slapped her bare bottom.

"Oooh, I like that," she cried, referring to his playful slap. "And besides, you are right. Sharing the shower is not a good thing. I would ravish your body and put you into a silly spin, as Andrew calls it," she replied, laughing.

Chapter Fifteen

They were out of the house and in the truck in record time to hit the road. At the bottom of the driveway, he gave her a blindfold and asked her to put it on until he told her to take it off. Hesitantly she obliged, trusting him. There was a little silence, only because she was trying to figure out where he was taking her. She was trying to decipher their locations by the directions that the truck would take.

"Okay, I can see that pretty little brain of yours at work. Stop trying to figure out where I am taking you, just sit back and enjoy the surprise. Do you think that you can do that for me?" he asked as he shot her a quick glance that she obviously could not see, but she felt it. She could always feel him watching her. It was like it had become her sixth sense. She loved how he made her feel.

They had been driving for a little while now. She had to ask. "All right, I'll behave, only because you asked nicely. Just one question and then I promise to be quiet."

"Just one, and it better not be where are we going!"

"Nope, won't ask that. How long before we get there? I have to go pee, I forgot to go before we left." She chuckled a little, not wanting to laugh too hard for fear of peeing her pants.

He let out a little laugh as well before he responded, "Not long, just up ahead, can you hold it that long?"

"Yes, thank you."

True to his word, within minutes, he put the truck into park. "Hold on, don't take it off yet, I will come around to get you."

He got out and walked around the truck to open up her door to help her out and walk her up to the cabin, where he had everyone waiting for her birthday dinner.

He opened the cabin door and led her through it. Reaching for the light switch, he turned it on, and just as he took off her blindfold, everyone yelled, "Surprise!"

She blinked and threw her hands up in the air then covered her mouth.

"You guys! I was wondering where everyone was today!" Andrew ran over to her to give her a big birthday hug and kiss. This was her family, and she was enjoying the surprise, but she really did have to go pee.

"Excuse me. I am really happy to see you all here, but I need the bathroom. Please point me in the right direction. And you! I love you!" She turned and looked at Rick briefly, awaiting direction to the bathroom, to which Andrew was happy to point and she was too happy to follow directions.

Rick said to everyone while waiting for Amy to return, "I really thought that you guys were going to give it away when she told me that there was no one at the house today. But she really didn't suspect a thing. Thank you."

They were at Elmhirst's Resort. This cabin was one of their honeymoon suites, and the dining room accommodated the five of them nicely. He was impressed with it. After all he only saw pictures online and booked it. It also contained three bedrooms, should they need it, but Philip assured him that they would not be staying the night, that it was all theirs to enjoy. Amy returned to the table, where everyone was waiting for dinner, and it arrived shortly. It was a delicious steak and lobster with roasted baby potatoes and fresh greens from their garden. To top dinner off, he had champagne for everyone. Of course, being pregnant, Sandra regretfully declined and enjoyed iced tea instead, and Andrew his milk.

Amy thanked everyone for helping her celebrate her birthday and wished everyone a happy Valentine's Day, with plenty more good things to happen for this family. Shortly after dinner, Philip announced that they were leaving and thanked Rick for the dinner and said the next one was on him, and for them to enjoy the rest of their night. Amy thanked everyone again for helping her celebrate her birthday. She gave everyone kisses good-bye with "see you tomorrow"s.

"How did you ever pull it off? Where was Sandi all day?" She turned to look at Rick, who had taken comfort on the big, comfy sofa.

"Why don't you come over here and let me wish you a proper happy birthday. Don't worry your pretty little head about how I pulled this off. If I told you how, I wouldn't be able to do it again," he said as he patted the seat beside him. She dutifully obeyed him with her head down as if she were pouting.

"I won't have any of that now, either. Come here, give me a big kiss. My arms have missed you," he said to her as she sat down, almost missing the couch but hitting his lap instead, which was not a big deal, as that was really where he wanted her anyway. He embraced her in his arms before his lips found hers. They hungrily met. He could still taste the champagne on her lips. She wiggled her body while still kissing him so that she was straddling his lap and her burning-with-desire crotch was pressing firmly against his growing groin.

She let a smile escape her lips, and with an obsession his tongue took hers. Her hands were entwined through his dark hair, rubbing his neck as he was lifting her top up over her head. She let go and broke their kiss long enough to allow the removal. Her breathing was long and heavy as she anticipated what she would like to happen next. His thumbs hooked under her bra straps to pull them down. He slid his hand onto her heaving chest and gently caressed her tits, index finger and thumb finding her anxiously waiting nipples. He first looked up into her face, and he recognized the signs of pleasure, as her head was tilted back, her eyes were closed, and she was biting her bottom lip. Her hands were resting, yet her fingernails were digging into his shoulders, and she was pressing her crotch harder against his throbbing groin. He had to slow this down. It was not quite what he had in mind for tonight. Yes, he wanted her, but he had other ideas of how to get here. He stopped cold.

She opened her eyes and looked down at him, waited a minute, then nothing. "Okay, what gives?" she asked with a puzzled tone.

"Nothing gives, baby. I just want tonight to be a night that you remember. We were moving too fast." Looking into her caring eyes, he had no problem telling her about a fantasy that he had, and he just hoped that she would be a willing participant. Having her still sitting on his lap, half-naked, was not helping his throbbing erection.

"Okay, but I'm not buying it. We have been having amazing lovemaking since Christmas. I bet that I could recite every time that we have made love. Can you?" Looking down into his mysterious dark eyes, she saw the hint of something else in mind there. "Spill. I have you captive."

"You always have me captive, and I cannot surrender anytime soon. I have this idea…that we could share our fantasies with each other tonight or at least talk about them. It's something that I have thought about but never addressed before." He spoke so softly, with a husky hint of sexy, and she could not help but inquire as to what he had in mind.

"What are you thinking? Or do you want me to go first? I have never spoken of this before, either. It was a topic that was forbidden in our house growing up." She still sat on his lap. His erection was not as pronounced. The mood had changed somewhat. There was this silence that was not disturbing or erotic, it was just silence.

She broke in first. "I've always liked dancing, and I thought that I would enjoy doing a striptease for my partner. I am most definitely comfortable with myself…" Just listening to her talk about doing a striptease was making him hard again, and he knew that she felt him hardening as she shifted and rubbed her crotch against him.

"Ohhh, baby doll…You have me so turned on. The erotic vision you just painted, I can get into that, it sort of goes with what I have imagined since we did the photo shoot for *Rustler,* which brings up my next surprise for you. You will find it in the master bedroom on the bed…" He didn't even get the last part out before she was up off his lap, trotting to the bedroom, leaving him fully aroused.

"Ahhhh…oh, my God" were noises coming from the bedroom. She had opened the package. It was a copy of her in *Rustler* and what he considered to be the sexiest turn-on piece of clothing that any woman could wear…a French maid's uniform complete with duster. He could hear her laughing in there.

"Is everything okay in there, or do I need to come in there?" he called in to her. It wasn't long before she came sauntering out in her new outfit. She took her duster and pretended to dust off the coffee table, leaning over with her back to him, giving him a nice view of her crotch. The outfit contained no panties, only the garter belt and the cap. He must say he did enjoy the view. Next she walked around the other side of the table, lifted her silk-stockinged leg, and placed it on the table, swinging it out and dropping a book on the floor…

"Ooops, pardon moi. Monsieur, can you please get that for moi?" she teased in a French little accent.

He obeyed. Leaning down to pick it up, he could not help but look up, and this was just a fantastic view and better than he had planned so far for a fantasy. He still had the book in his hand as he straightened out, and she seductively swayed her hips as she walked over and straddled his lap.

"Does monsieur like l'outfit?" She leaned into him, pressing her bosom against his hard chest. She could feel his breathing becoming rapid. He leaned his face toward her, going to steal a kiss, but she stopped him by shaking her head, taking the book from his hands, and bringing them up over his head, holding them there with one hand.

"No, no, no, monsieur, we must be patient…"

He never in his wildest dreams thought it could get any better with her. She was so hot in this French maid outfit.

"But, mon cherie, I am the boss. This is not acceptable behaviour." He went along with the seduction, and in one quick swoop took charge of the situation. He now had her arms behind her back, holding them with his left hand, leaving his right to go around her waist as he just as quickly changed their position. He was now positioned on top of her on the overly big sofa. The look of surprise on her face told him that she, too, was enjoying this little adventure. He let go of her arms so that he could seductively massage her tits that were practically overflowing the costume. He lifted one out and her nipple was taut. He continued to pinch and pull on it with his thumb and forefinger. He felt her shiver with desire as anticipation was starting to overwhelm them. He aggressively took possession of her mouth in a hot kiss, and she refused at first, shaking her head.

"No, no, no, monsieur," she tried saying as his tongue invaded her moist, warm mouth and found her tongue excitedly ready to please. He felt her wetness as he pressed his achingly hard erection against her. She was letting out little moans as he continued to kiss her with passion that filled him. She could feel his heart pounding as his chest was pressed up against hers, nearly in time with the throbbing between her thighs. She slid her hand down between them and awkwardly unzipped his pants, reaching in to release his cock. It was hard and pulsing in her hand, demanding action as it reached freedom. He pushed himself closer to her, moaning as it found her hot, wet pussy. His cock still in her hand, she rubbed him back and forth against her, and he groaned with desire. He seductively caressed his hand down her side and her leg before he lifted it to better position himself.

"Mon cherie, moi cannot take much more, you are driving me insane," he whispered into her ear, and that sent more goose bumps through her. A low moan escaped from deep down inside her as his lips blazed a trail down her neck just as he thrust himself deep inside her center. Her entire body was on fire. He could feel it, too. She was crying out his name as his rhythm increased. Pumping, he was losing himself in the moment. He felt her muscles tighten around him. She now had both her legs wrapped around his waist with her ankles locked together. She lifted her ass up off the sofa as he slid his hands around her slender waist, pulling her into him. He was almost ready to explode. She tightened again and, flexing her inner muscles, she let out a moderate scream as she climaxed. That did it for him, with one more deep, pulsating thrust. He stopped and surrendered to the moment. Her arms fell limp beside them, and she loosed her legs around him.

"Monsieur, your wife will be home any moment, no?" She continued their little charade, looking directly into his eyes, and she saw something, pleasure, warmth, and love like never before.

"Mon cherie, no fear of her finding out, as you will be my wife." He said it with such tender, loving words that a tear escaped her eye. She was so much in love with him that she would do anything for him. She leaned up into him to give him a kiss, and she watched him as they kissed tenderly for a moment before he broke away entirely.

He stood up from the sofa, extending his hand to help her up, and she could not stop admiring this man that she loved. She noticed his semierection and she knew that this night was not over by a long shot. She took his hand, and he led her to the bedroom without another word spoken. He seductively released her from her uniform and gently pushed her back to fall onto the bed, where she wiggled her way up and propped herself up onto her elbows to watch. He sexily undressed before her, slowly releasing his big strong arms from his shirt, undoing the button to his jeans, and seductively sliding them and his boxers to the floor. He was fully aroused again, ready for round two. He stood before her naked.

"Oh, babe, so big and strong. Come to Momma," she seductively teased, and he joined her on the bed, where they made passionate love again and again that night. Both their bodies were covered with sweat from their lovemaking. It was the wee hours of the morning, and they had not yet slept. She rolled over to look at him resting. His eyes were closed but not sleeping, and she ran her fingernail across his flat nipple to get his attention.

"Are you ready for round ninety-four?" he asked teasingly with his eyes still shut.

"Not quite yet. How did I rate for your fantasy last night? Did I do a good job, monsieur?" she asked as she threw her arm over his heavy chest.

"Babe, you were out of this world last night. I never fantasized that it would be that amazing. When do we get to fulfill yours?" He opened his eyes to admire his equal in every sense of the word.

"I will let you know. For now, I need some rest. My thighs are aching. I can't remember using them so much. Thank you for a wonderful birthday that I will truly remember for a lifetime." Smiling, she placed a sweet, gentle kiss on his lips before laying her head down onto his chest to catch a few winks.

It had felt like she just closed her eyes when she felt the bed move. Lazily, she opened them, and she rubbed them to help focus then heard Rick's voice. He was talking on his cell phone. She sat up in bed for few minutes before she decided to climb into the shower. She picked up her watch on the nightstand to see what time it was…holy cow, it was 10:30 a.m. She had slept six hours. He heard her gasp for air, and he quickly turned to look at her shaking her head in disbelief. Looking at her, he mouthed the words, "give me a minute," pointing to his phone.

"Not a problem," she whispered back and pointed to the shower. She had noticed that he was already dressed, his hair damp, which meant that he must have already had his shower. He must have been anxious to get on the road and head back to the ranch. There were still things that needed to be done before they headed out at the end of April for the Kentucky Derby.

They had purchased, last fall, a new racehorse. Her name was Pride, from a ranch that was going under. Pride had won the Kentucky Derby twice in a row about four years ago but had an accident and the owner felt that she was not worth it to retrain and keep racing. After looking at her, Rick knew that she still had it in her, she wasn't that old, still a young mare. Bob was helping in the retraining and exercising her, and the last that Philip had mentioned they found a jockey that could get her to the finish line. His name was Tommy Hicks, a bright and easygoing guy that had experience and believed that he could help them get the ranch a win at the Kentucky Derby.

She came out of the shower feeling refreshed, and she found Rick sitting on the sofa, browsing through the February issue of *Rustler*…She snuck up behind him. "I thought that you didn't look at smut rags?" she teasingly said as she wrapped her arms around his neck from behind and gave the top of his head a peck, then rubbed her hands on his cheeks…

"More than a five o'clock shadow, darlin'!"

He reached over and pulled her into his lap across the low back of the sofa. "Only when they show such a beautiful specimen do I engage in such smut…" He laughed as he set it down.

"I would like to head out in a little bit, if that is okay with you? Bob is running into some issues with Pride. I want you to know that last night was amazing, and we still need to address yours, and I won't forget." He planted a loving kiss on her lips.

"I am ready whenever you are, and don't worry, I won't let monsieur forget either."

Shortly after that, they packed up the truck. He grabbed his Stetson and placed it on her head as he led her out to the truck to head for home. She told him that they would have to remember this place and come back often. She truly enjoyed herself, and it was the best birthday she had had in years. They talked about her next assignment in Hawaii and how she really wanted him to join her. He told her that they would discuss it some more later, but right now he didn't see how it was possible for him to get away for a couple of days let alone a week.

Chapter Sixteen

They had some fun times, playful times, and after the guys left for dinner some nights they would play about in the stalls. It was some of the best lovemaking that she ever experienced. It could have been the thrill of possibly getting caught in the act, she didn't know.

He had showed her how Mystery was becoming sulky and that this was her "season" and it was time to introduce her to Sir Lancelot. It was also time to get the vet out there to help in the process. She was so impressed and excited to watch and be part of this process. Her father never really let the girls have any part of this. He was kind of old-fashioned. He wanted them to grow up and find husbands that would run his ranch.

They were going to sell the foals from Mystery and Sir Lancelot, since both had great racing bloodlines in their genes.

She managed to get the caterer booked for the wedding, along with the officiate, and next week invitations would be ready at the printers.

Before she knew it, March was here. She had been trying to give Sandra as much time and space as she needed to finish studying for her bar exam. To some degree Amy was a little jealous of her big sister for her accomplishments. She had taken the time to get a degree, was married to a wonderful man, okay not that part, but she had a wonderful son and a baby on the way. Not just any degree, but she studied to become a lawyer. That was the part that she mostly envied. She wished that she had taken the time to do some studying. The problem was she was never really interested in school, and she never really knew what she "wanted to be when she grew up"...how cliché was that? Here she was, all grown up, she had a fabulous fiancé who adored her, and if she still wanted it, a fabulous career. She still had one more assignment to do before she was to announce to the world that she was giving it all up. Maybe she could change her mind.

Things were too chaotic after the beginning of the year. It was time to get things packed up for Hawaii. That was where they were sending her for her next assignment. It was only a two-day gig. This time it was for a conversation dialogue in a forum with Madeline Principal. Just after the *Rustler* assignment, Sophie had sent her this package of cosmetic creams and blemish concealers, et cetera, to use, advising that her March assignment in Hawaii was to meet with Madeline and go over the changes that her products had made to her complexion. This was something totally different than she had ever done before.

Things had slowed down at the ranch. Felix said that he could run things for a couple of weeks, should they decide to stay down there for a few extra days. And it appeared that Bob had things once again under control with Pride and training her was back on track. She liked this new guy, Tommy. He had a way with Pride, they seemed to connect, and from what she had been reading in the books about racing thoroughbreds it was important that the jockey and the horse were compatible. Rick told her that he was impressed with everything that she was learning and enjoyed having her down there.

On the flight down there, they talked again about how the house was getting too small for everyone that lived in it. They still had lots of land to the west of the house, "Why don't we build a small bungalow there?" he asked her as the plane was coming in for a landing.

"I think that would be a fantastic idea, I agree that the house is too small for all of us there, Sandra will have her hands full once baby 'dunno' arrives." She chuckled. "Dunno" was what Andrew was calling the baby. Dunno, meaning he didn't know if he wanted a baby sister or baby brother. He started school in January, part-time, three full days and half the day on Fridays.

The shuttle drove them over to the hotel in Maui, and they checked into the honeymoon suite despite the fact that they were not married yet. It was a sweet oversight. But they planned to enjoy it anyway.

Her first meeting was with Ms. Principal this afternoon. Her chauffeur was due in twenty minutes to pick her up.

"Are you going to be all right while I go over to the studio? I shouldn't be that long, and then the rest of the day is ours," she asked him as they were putting some clothes away. Rick had gone over to the French doors to open them and enjoy the view.

"I will be fine here. I am sure that I can find a few things to amuse myself…Hey, look, there is a hot chick on the beach. Maybe I will go over and introduce myself…" he commented in a joking tone. She walked over to him and gave him a hug from behind.

"It's only two days of work then I am all yours…"

"Honey, you are all mine anyway. But I will manage. I agreed to come. I knew that it had some work involved. I don't really want to be sitting in that stuffy studio twiddling my thumbs."

She reluctantly left when the front desk called to advise that her driver was here. Out of all the famous people that she had met during her career, Madeline Principal was right up on top of her list. Madeline's outlook on life and ambitions inspired Amy's dreams. And being able to finally meet this woman was a dream come true.

The next two days were a whirlwind for Amy, spending time with Madeline talking about her cosmetic line and how it worked and felt, as well as many other topics. She promised to have Amy return for an update on the product use and how she was enjoying married life.

For the first time that she could remember, she woke up feeling a little under the weather, sick to her stomach, just the overall feeling of nausea overwhelmed her. As Rick went to get some juice and soda crackers, she laid there in bed…

"When was the last time that I had my period? Since being with Rick, I do not recall once that we used protection. Oh, my God! No, it can't be happening, could it?"

She didn't even hear Rick return until he asked, "What can't be happening?" She didn't want to say anything until she knew for sure that he wanted kids and that she was pregnant. She scrambled to cover up what she didn't realize was loud enough for someone else to hear.

"I can't be sick now. This is a special time for us. There are so many things that I would like for us to explore and do here on Maui." She looked at him with loving eyes as he handed her the juice and crackers.

After about an hour's worth of rest, she was feeling much better, but the thought that she might be pregnant was still in the back of her mind. The waters were beautiful, the wind in her hair, the feel of the water splashing on her face, they even saw a whale or two while they took a sail out on one of the Hawaiian canoes. After that, they took a long, romantic walk along the beautiful beach. They reached the hotel, and she excused herself briefly to go into the hotel's pharmacy. She needed to pick up some personal items, she told him. Without another thought or word, he bent and kissed her just before he boarded the elevator to their suite.

She went in and picked up the item that she wanted along with a few other items. From reading the instructions, she had another day to wait before she could take the test, and it worked best first thing in the morning. She found him out on the lanai leaning on the railing. His strong quadriceps, big strong shoulders, and biceps were all visible since he had taken off his shirt and his legs were stretched out behind him. Oh, how he made her yearn for him just by being there. She was glad that he was hers and hers alone. He did not hear her come into the suite, and it wasn't until she was standing in the French doorway that he realized she was back…"I hear you breathing…" he commented as she continued to approach.

"I didn't realize that my breathing was that loud," she said as she slipped her arm through his that was resting on the railing to stand beside him.

"It's not that it's loud, I just have this radar whenever you come around me. I sense you near and my body gets this..."

She finished his sentence, "Tingling sensation, a feeling of desire overwhelms you."

"Yes, that's it...Have I told you lately how much I love you?" he replied in a husky, raspy voice.

"Not in the last hour. I could never hear it enough. I want you so bad right now. Do you know that?" She lifted his arm up so that she could crawl under it to stand between him and the railing, turning to face him.

She took her hands and started caressing his chest, her thumbs lightly over his flat nipples, and then her mouth hungrily reached up to take his. He liked this side of her, the taking charge. He could almost get used to it. She backed him up until he plunked down on the lounge chair, where she straddled him, not losing a beat in their hot, tingling kiss. His hands now cupped her bottom as she rubbed her aching center onto his bulging groin. She now placed soft little nips over his ears and down his neck, and when she stopped to run her tongue over his nipples, he let out soft, pleasuring moans. He untied her bikini top and let it fall forward. His eyes fell to her chest, admiring her large, firm bosom and taut nipples that were begging him to touch. They shared amazing lovemaking out on the lanai that night.

She didn't remembering making it to the bed last night or if they even stopped for dinner, but there they were the next morning. As he was snuggled up close to her, she felt his erection pressing against her thigh. She had to go to the bathroom, slinking across the king-size bed so as not to disturb him. Remembering the instructions from the pregnancy test that she had to use her first morning urine to test, she held the stick into her pee stream. It took ten minutes for the test. She stayed in the bathroom, occasionally looking out to see if he woke up. Nope, still asleep. It felt like the longest ten minutes of her life. She heard him rustle on the bed, and she quickly tossed the evidence into the trash, grabbing the stick and reading it, talking softly to herself, "Single blue line not pregnant, double pink lines—pregnant. It's a double pink line. We are pregnant!" Panic and happiness were emotions that overcame her all at once, and she barely heard him when he called out to her…

"Ames? Are you here?" She came charging in from the bathroom, holding the positive stick behind her back. "What's you got, girl?" He tried to get it from her as she jumped back onto the bed, wearing this excited, silly grin on her face. "What's with you?" He stopped trying to get whatever it was she was hiding.

She brought it out, waving it around, and he caught a faint glimpse of the stick. Not being certain of exactly what she was waving, he grabbed her wrist to stop the movement. He knew now what she held. He looked at her with his own mischievous smile, almost as if he knew it was bound to happen sooner or later. They had been having unprotected sex for months, and if he had to be completely honest, he did not feel one bit guilty. He wanted to have lots of children with this woman.

"I can only assume that this look of excitement is because we're about to have a baby?"

Still holding her wrist in his hand, she threw her other one around his neck and pulled him into her, whispering, "Yes…we are going to have a baby of our own." Leaning back to look into his face again, trying to read him, she said, "Are you okay with that? I mean, we have not talked about the possibility before. Nor have we ever once mentioned the use of protection of any kind."

"It just means that we should push the wedding date up and really need to start on that house of ours sooner rather than later…The next question is how far along do you suspect we are?" He was holding her in his arms. He was ecstatic over this news. He always wanted a family of his own. Being a little naive, he just thought that they would have had some time to enjoy being husband and wife first. He looked at her with adoration.

"I'm really not sure. I don't recall having my period since December—before Christmas. So we could be talking about two…two and half months? I will make an appointment as soon as we get back, to confirm everything. So are you okay with this? Are we okay?" Concern really overtook her. He could see it in her face. The rest of his comment had not even really sunk in yet with her. He just told her that they should get married before June. He couldn't stand the thought of her being in such distress.

"Baby, we are better than okay. I love you, and I am in complete adoration of the fact that we might be having a little one of our own." He paused before he told her a little secret of his own that he had all arranged the day before.

"We are going to get married this afternoon down on the beach. I made the arrangements the other day while you were at the studio. It was supposed to be a surprise. But I guess yours outweighs mine." He let out a little laugh as he tickled her sides, hoping to lighten her mood and confirm to her that he was all right with this new revelation of hers.

She squirmed under his touch. It sent a burning desire that she felt all the way down her body, and just then she also felt a wave of nausea. This must be the morning sickness that Sandra was feeling in her early stages, she thought…She quickly pushed his hands away to jump up and run to the bathroom.

He heard her vomiting. Suddenly he felt like a heel, but he didn't want to wait now until June to marry her, and he really was not about to apologize for that. He got up and went into the bathroom. He knelt down and held her hair away from her face as she threw up again. He grabbed the washcloth from the basin and rinsed it with cool water and dabbed her forehead, just before she threw up again…

“Thanks, but you don’t need to be in here,” she said as she reached to remove his hand and threw up again.

“I want to help you every step of the way through this. I brought this on, did this to you.” He was being such a sap and a gentleman at the same time, she loved that about him, but to her this was embarrassing, having a loved one watch as you hurl into the toilet bowl. She waved her hand again and asked him to just leave her alone. Reluctantly, he got up and left the room. While she was still in there, he ordered them some breakfast, mainly toast, juice, and some fruit, not really knowing what she would feel like when she came out. A few minutes later she emerged from the bathroom and splashed some cool water on her face, which helped her feel better.

Chapter Seventeen

"I'm sorry for kicking you out of the bathroom. It's embarrassing to have someone watch as you hurl, at least it is to me. I understand that you only wanted to help." She paused as she looked around and saw the nice table set up for breakfast, and suddenly she felt like a jerk. She walked over to him and put her arms around his waist. A feeling of panic overtook her, as he didn't immediately put his around her. She felt him tense. She backed away from him to look at him and try to read whatever the message was that he was trying to send to her. She was confused. He stood there just like a statue, no expression on his face.

She had to lighten the mood. It got way too heavy in the room, so she poked him in the gut. He let out a breath of air, and a huge smile filled his face. She felt a wave of relief come over her. He then reached out and took her arm and pulled her to him to embrace, and he kissed the top of her head as he brushed his hand down her hair and rubbed her back before he cupped her ass. Something that he loved to do was hold her ass in his hands. It just felt so right. She let out a little giggle.

"Okay, so we are getting married this afternoon. How much time do I have to get ready?" She raised her head to look up at him.

"Oh, about two hours. We are scheduled to be on the beach at 1:00 p.m.," he responded as he looked at the nightstand clock. "Why don't you go down to the boutique and buy yourself something pretty to wear that will make you feel comfortable. Have your hair done, too!" he said as he handed her his Platinum Visa card. Without another look, she grabbed it and started to walk toward the door to go…She was playing with him. "Ummm, babe, don't you think that you are forgetting something important?"

He really didn't think that she would leave the room naked, but stranger things had been known to happen. She stopped dead in her tracks, looked around the room for a moment and spun around on her heel to look at him with a puzzled expression on her face, her bottom lip sucked in. "Ah, I don't think so." He waved his hand down his body. He had on only his robe, and the gesture indicated that she wasn't quite dressed appropriately to leave the room. She looked down, and a surprised expression overcame her face.

"Ooops, I guess that I need to get dressed first." She laughed at him, like a "yeah, I knew, just trying to get to you" kind of laugh.

She walked over to the dresser to get a T-shirt and pair of shorts to put on, and as she was getting dressed she thought that she better ask him what he was planning on wearing so that she would know what to get for herself. Though she already had an idea of what she wanted to wear. "What do you plan on wearing for the ceremony?" She looked at him as she continued to get ready to leave.

"I have a pair of dress pants and a Hawaiian shirt, not loud, white with soft greens. Does that help you decide on what to wear?"

"Yup…I still think that my birthday suit would be great, but not so great for the wedding album…hehehe." She plunked a kiss on his cheek, and he swatted her bottom as she turned to leave.

After she left, he got himself dressed and left the room. He had one final thing to do before the ceremony. He went to the jewelers to have her wedding band engraved "2G4E-Craig." It was the ultimate gift that he could give to her, especially now that she was pregnant.

She was having the time of her life here in Hawaii at the boutique, and she bought a beautiful red, white-orchid-panel, spaghetti-strap muumuu. It was full-length with a little ruffle at the bust. She decided not to wear any shoes. It was the beach. Then she went over to have her hair done. She showed them her dress so that they had an idea of how to do her hair. They decided on an updo with cascading curls down her back and sides to show off her lovely shoulders along with a traditional white-orchid haku around her head. The salon took a snapshot for her keepsake, and she thanked everyone for their help in getting her ready.

She left the salon with a giddy feeling. They were actually going to do this, get married. A wave of guilt suddenly overcame her, thinking about the invitations and the rest of the arrangements that had already been done back home. She pushed that out of her mind. They would deal with that when they got home.

She arrived back at their room to find it empty with only a note on the table where also rested a beautiful bouquet of calla lilies. She talked to herself as she read the note…"He really did think of everything. 'You are the most beautiful woman that I have ever had the privilege of knowing. Here is your bouquet, and once you are ready there is a limo waiting for you outside the hotel. It will bring you to me. Where we will start our life together. I love you, Ames! Love, Rick." How sweet. She quickly got into her dress, grabbed a pair of high-heeled, white sandals that she had brought with her since she really wasn't planning on wearing any shoes and her bouquet, and headed for the limo. She sat quietly in the limo as it drove her to the location, and then the driver helped her out of the car, finding Rick waiting for her as the limo pulled up.

As she stepped out of the limo, his jaw dropped. "You like what you see, I take it?" She smiled at him. With her shoes on, she came almost eye to eye with him. He took her hand and wrapped the other free arm around her still-tiny waist as he walked her to the beach. The photographer stopped them a couple of times to take a few pictures. It was a beautiful day in their paradise. It was sunny, not too bright that it would be blinding, and there was a soft breeze off the water with waves lapping on shore. They reached their officiant, introductions were made, and Rick turned to face Amy to say their vows. She was lost in a small trance as she looked at him. Here was this handsome, incredibly well-built man who had a heart of gold, and he wanted her.

They said their vows, and when the officiate gave her his ring, he had to show her what he had engraved. She was so touched that she had to refrain from hugging him before she was allowed to. They exchanged their rings and were pronounced husband and wife, and he could now kiss his bride. His kiss was seductive and amazingly hot. It was just a sample of what was waiting for her back at their hotel room. They had a few more pictures taken before he had the limo take them back to the hotel.

They arrived back at the hotel to have a romantic dinner waiting for them out on the lanai. With the sun setting and soft, beautiful music, she was truly impressed with all the arrangements and care that he took in setting this up. He walked her out to the table and pulled out her chair for her to sit. They had casual conversation over dinner, talking about the wonderful experiences that they shared here on the island of paradise, and they talked about the unexpected pregnancy. They even talked about how they were going to break it to the family when they returned. It was decided that they would keep their original plans for the wedding back home, as it was arranged to have his real name printed on their marriage certificate, even though this day would always be their anniversary, March 26.

After dinner, he poured them a nice relaxing bubble bath and opened the doors to enjoy the ocean view from the Jacuzzi tub, where he washed her in the most sensual, sexy way that she had ever enjoyed. He took special care drying her off before he carried her off to their bed, where he made wonderful, passionate love to her for hours. Their lovemaking was a sedative.

It did not take long for Rick to fall off to sleep that night. She laid there for a while longer as things crowded her mind…She was thinking that she was not too bright. She should have recognized the signs of this pregnancy or, one better, they should have used protection. She had noticed that her clothes were fitting a little tighter than normal and her skin had a special glow to it, but she should have noticed her missed periods. Most of all, she was really happy about this pregnancy. She would have it confirmed when they returned home. Lying next to her husband gave her the sense of comfort and security that had been missing in her life. She loved him so.

They stayed in Maui a few more days enjoying the sunshine, the water, and their private time together, as they knew that once they returned to Soul's Valley their time alone would be limited to their bedroom.

They were waiting at the airport to board their plane when Rick saw him. He was standing over at the newsstand. He was never more certain of anything before. Sontiago's son was at this airport, and he could not risk being seen. It had been a long time, but his buddies at the FBI said not to risk it, since they no longer followed him on a regular basis. He quickly turned around but not so that he drew attention to himself. Just then he heard their flight being called to boarding.

He reached for Amy's arm and her carry-on bag. "Just act normally, like there is nothing wrong. Casually turn your head. Do you see the man with the cigar standing over at the newsstand?"

She was confused just a bit but soon realized that it only meant one thing, so she casually turned to look. "Yeah, I see him. He's talking to another guy."

"Are they coming this way?" he asked as they stopped at the desk for the stewardess to check their tickets. He looked at Amy as he released his hold on her arm. He had a sick feeling come over him. For the first time in twenty years, he felt scared. It wasn't for himself, now it was for his wife and his unborn child. These men would stop at nothing. He caught a glimpse himself. They were not following them. Did he get himself caught up in the past? He didn't know. Maybe they didn't recognize him?

"Rick…You are scaring me. You don't think that they recognized you, do you? I don't see them following us," she asked as they walked to the plane.

"I honestly don't know…I'm sorry that I have scared you. That is the last thing that I ever wanted to do." He squeezed her tighter against him as they walked onboard the plane. They found their seats in first class. He took another look around to see if he could see anything that might look out of place. He didn't see anything, but he was far from experienced in this. He really didn't know what to look for. A man that he recognized from the hotel walked slowly by as they took their seats and flashed his jacket to show an FBI badge. That alarmed him, but he continued to try and hold back his anxiety. He didn't want to scare Amy any more than he already had.

She was really worried that perhaps she had done something to bring this on. Did she really try hard enough to keep him out of the media, could she have done a better job? These were all thoughts that were going through her mind as they sat there waiting for takeoff.

Looking at her, he said, "Ames…it's going to be okay. I promise. Give me a kiss." He leaned into her to help soften the moment and ease her mind, and she turned to him and gave him what he wanted, a kiss. It wasn't anything to write home about, it was just that, a kiss. Simple, a little linger, but there was no spark. What happened to their spark? It was just this morning that she knew that they had it. Fear had a way of changing everything.

"Rick…I need to know, did I do this? I don't want anything to happen to you. I thought that I was doing a good job of keeping your picture from the media?" she asked with this look of sorrow in her eyes. He did not like that look. He was going to fix this right now. He was going back there to talk to the feds.

Just then one of the stewardesses asked him to follow her. "It's going to be all right. I promise. I will be right back." Giving her another kiss, this was sending her a message that he would do whatever it was that he had to do to protect them. He left with the woman, and she sat there and sat there, waiting. Ten minutes had passed, and the captain had asked that everyone buckle up, that they were heading up the runway. Rick still had not returned yet.

She didn't know why, but she felt the urge to look around her surroundings. She felt like someone was watching her, and it was an eerie feeling. Was this what it was like growing up for him, constantly looking over your shoulder? Just as he had expressed his fears or doubts about fitting into her way of life, she was starting to have doubts of her own of fitting into his way of life. She was someone famous with her picture constantly in the media, could she really do this? Become a nobody to protect their family from harm? The answer was yes, yes she could and would do anything to protect what she found with Rick.

They were on their way home and could move freely amongst the plane, and she thought about going to look for Rick when this man approached her and asked her for her autograph. That didn't happen a lot to her, so she was a bit overwhelmed by the attention.

Chapter Eighteen

Meanwhile, Rick was in the galley talking to the feds.

"Rick, we need for you to act like nothing is out of the ordinary. We have followed one of Sontiago's men here only to learn that he has set up a ring in Maui. We really don't feel that you are in any danger, that they are not looking for you or your family. And we don't think that they even recognized you. We learned yesterday that Sontiago arrived here the day after you and your wife. The two of you had passed a number of times at the hotel and the mall, yet he never gave you a second look. Just play it cool. We only put surveillance on you as a precautionary measure," Agent Rinaldi was telling him. The agent's reassurance did not make him feel any better.

"Has there been any buzz since the media took our pictures after Christmas in New York? Amy has fears that she has put me in danger, and I need to reassure her that it's not the case. Can I do that?" he asked as he began to stand.

"Rick, like I said, he didn't look twice at you the whole time you shared the same hotel. We are pretty confident that your father's case twenty years ago is just that, a history case. I wouldn't go out and advertise that you were Craig. Let sleeping dogs lie. Your family is as safe as who you have been the last twenty years," Rinaldi said in an undertone, leaning in toward Rick, making sure that prying ears were not listening.

Rick reached for Agent Rinaldi's hand to give him a firm handshake and thank him for protecting him and his family. He left the agent sitting in the galley. He arrived back at his seat to find another man sitting next to his wife. They were talking, and she held a magazine in her lap. As he got closer he recognized it to be the February issue of *Rustler*. This he was not prepared for. Looking at the two of them together, she let out a little laugh. It almost irritated him, but he put his anger aside for the moment to find out what was so funny.

"Hey there, sweetie. I see that we found our favourite magazine?" Looking at the two of them, she looked up at him to see that he was not entirely pleased to find this fan sitting in his place or with the fact that they had the centerfold page open.

"Rick, honey…this is Leo Pane. He just happened to recognize me from our favourite pose…" She again let out a little giggle. "He asked me to autograph my behind for him. I didn't see any reason why I couldn't oblige." Turning her attention back to Leo, she said, "Thank you for the kind words, Leo, and I wish you and your wife all the best and hope that your little girl gets her wish for a little brother. When did you say your wife was due again?" She tried to lighten the mood around the three of them.

Taking the magazine back, he told them that she was due in May and again thanked Amy for her kindness then returned to his seat.

"I do believe that is the first time that I have seen the green-eyed monster come out in you. I really don't like him," she said in a matter-of-fact tone and looked away into the window. He sat down beside her, trying to find the words to talk to her. She was right, he had been jealous of the man that sat next to his wife. He really didn't like that man, either. He knew that he had nothing to worry about, that he should expect that sort of thing. He did marry a famous, fabulous, drop-dead-gorgeous woman, and she chose him to spend the rest of her life with. He reached for her hand, which she had crossed over her chest, as he took her hand into his. His thumb traced her erect nipple. The touch sent an electrifying, sensuous thrill through her body from her head to her toes. The feeling was back. It wasn't lost. She couldn't help but turn and look at him. She could never stay angry with him.

"You are absolutely right. I was jealous when I saw Mr. Leo leaning in on you and you were laughing. I didn't like it, and I could have handled it a little better. I am sorry…" He now had his hand on her chin. "Please forgive me. I promise that I will try harder in the future to not let him come out." He looked into her eyes, searching for the response that he wanted, that it was okay to kiss her. There it is, he thought to himself as he leaned into her and planted one of his soft, subtle kisses on her hot, tantalizing lips, lips that were telling him that she wanted more than just a kiss. He broke away first. "I will make full restitution when we get home," he said with a smile that told her that he would indeed. She laughed gently at his comment.

"I will hold you to that, Mr. Durham. I will expect it in full." She was giving him the once-over look then rested her eyes on his crotch. He noticed her advances as she slid her hand down to cup his groin and give it a playful squeeze.

He quickly placed the pillow into his lap. He was not one to give a public display, and his growing erection from her touch was doing just that. As he looked at her lovingly, he gently took her hand from his crotch and placed it on his armrest. "Darling, we can't do that here. It is not fair game."

"There is always the washroom?" She playfully smiled at him as she revealed a little more of her cleavage in his direction.

"Stop that!" He pulled her shirt back over her bosoms. "We're in a public place. What got into you?" He wasn't sure if he liked this playful side of her or not, but he knew that he was not comfortable in displaying this kind of affection in a public place. Holding hands and a kiss was okay. He felt the tension rise between them. He also noticed how she started to nervously fidget in her seat. She wouldn't look at him, and her cheeks were becoming flushed. From her profile he could also see the tears well in her eyes. *Oh, God, I hate it when she cries.* His heart just fell.

With a soft sob, she spoke. "I'm scared, Rick…" She was still looking out the plane window. She didn't like being this vulnerable.

These were feelings that she was not used to sharing with anyone else before. She could not bear it if she had put him in danger. For the first time since she realized that she could be pregnant, she ran her hand over her stomach as if to acknowledge the life growing inside her. She couldn't stand it. She had to turn and look at him. He was staring at her. Love and passion were shown on his face. His eyes had become sad.

Without another word said, he embraced her and rubbed her back and smoothed her hair over her shoulder. "There, there, baby, it'll be okay. I'm sorry if I did this to you." The sincerity was in his voice, and she again looked up into his eyes.

"You didn't do anything to me. It's me that has done this to you. I brought these bad people into our lives. I am so sorry, how can you ever forgive me?" She started to sob. It had to be the hormones kicking in, and this was completely out of character for her.

"What are you talking about? You didn't bring any danger into my life. I knew what I was getting into when I decided to pursue you. I talked to the guys, and everything is okay. We have nothing to worry about. He did not recognize me, and as long as we stay cool and act normal…as normal as we can be," he said with a small hint of sarcasm in his voice, hoping to relieve some of her worries.

The tension dissipated from her. He felt it as she started to relax. She fell asleep in his arms. He didn't have the heart to wake her until they arrived at JFK Airport. They were quiet the rest of the ride, and it was late when they arrived at home. They just left their suitcases on the bedroom floor and climbed into bed. He needed to get some rest. They were still having issues with the new mare. She was not cooperating with the training that he had set out for her, and he needed to get down there first thing in the morning. They didn't have much more time before the race on May 1.

Amy woke and noticed that Rick had been doing quite a bit of tossing and turning. Something was still bothering him. She noticed that he did that when he had something on his mind and didn't talk about it. She couldn't sleep anymore, as she must have had several hours' sleep on the plane. It was almost three in the morning. Carefully getting up so as not to disturb his sleep, she moved over to the chair to sit and watch him as he slept. The alarm went off at five thirty. She couldn't get to it fast enough. He stirred, rolling over to put his arm around her to find that she was not there. He immediately sat up and looked around the room only to find her sitting in the big chair.

"Baby…why aren't you here in bed with me? Come back to bed. You need your rest." He patted the bed then rubbed his eyes as he swung his legs over the edge of the bed.

"I couldn't sleep anymore. Are you going to tell me the truth about those men we saw in Hawaii and what the feds had to say on the plane?" She stood up to greet him a good morning as he, too, stood from the bed, stretching his arms over his head before he wrapped them around her.

"I told you last night that we have nothing to worry about. Agent Rinaldi had put a tail on us as a precaution when they learned that Sontiago's son had set up an operation in Maui. Apparently we passed each other a number of times at the hotel and he didn't even recognize me. The feds are not worried about our safety, so neither should we. We continue to live our lives. Does that satisfy your pretty little mind?" He kissed the top of her head before he pulled her down onto the bed with him as he fell backward. They lay there a few minutes on their sides before she spoke again.

"If we don't have anything to worry about, what has got you so upset? I watched as you slept. You did a lot of tossing and turning. You only sleep restlessly if you have something on your mind. I don't like to press, but I am sensing that we need to start to trust each other more and tell each other everything. I don't want any secrets. I love you and this baby, and I want us to start off right." She looked into his eyes, still searching for his answer.

"Okay, I agree, we do need to share everything with each other. It has nothing to do with Sontiago and his men. I talked to Bob again yesterday just before we left Maui. Pride is still not cooperating with her training. I can't figure it out. Her regiment is not that hard for the guys to follow, nor do I believe that it would push her too hard. And I love you and our baby!"

Pulling her closer to him, he slid his hand up underneath her robe to caress her bare skin. It was warm and inviting. The things that they could do, he thought as he felt his arousal. He glanced at the clock. Nope, no time for that. Instead he satisfied himself with a quick slap on her ass, and she let out a little yip as she placed a lingering kiss on his lips before she pushed him back.

"All right, I can live with that. What can I do to help?" she asked as she watched him getting up and walking toward the bathroom to shower. He turned to her.

"Nothing right at the moment. I need to go down there and assess the situation. Why don't you bring me down some lunch and we can talk about it in the office." He winked at her as he turned around.

He was in the shower as she suddenly felt the nausea overcome her, and she ran to the toilet and retched. It was the dry heaves. She hadn't had anything to eat or really drink since lunch yesterday. She just finished as he turned off the water. She flushed and sat up as he got out of the shower. Looking at her, he made a statement rather than a question. "Morning sickness." He rubbed her back as she washed her face. They got dressed and sauntered downstairs to join the others for breakfast. Anna should have it ready by now. It was just after seven in the morning. They found Sandra and Philip lounging over their coffees. Before they took their respective seats, Rick drew Amy into his arms as he spoke. "Do you want to tell them or shall I?" He looked at her then around the table.

"Tell us what? What have you two been up to? Did you enjoy Maui?" Sandra piped in, looking at the pair. She noticed the mischievous look on Rick's face.

Amy looked at her sister then her husband and burst out, "We got married in Maui!" She flung her ring hand out to show it with a giggle, again looking at Rick with a quick shake to tell him not to say a word about the pregnancy just yet. She caught his nod of approval.

"The wedding that you had planned is only a couple of months away. Why the rush? I don't understand…unless…" she looked at Amy then again at Rick then she turned to Philip. "Amy's pregnant!" She pushed her chair back and came around the table to embrace the couple. "I am so happy for you guys." It had been years since she could read her sister, but she knew that she hit the nail on the head with this one.

Rick shook his head in disbelief. "I'm not sure that I even want to question how you figured that out, but I just couldn't stand the thought that I couldn't have her to myself. I'm an old-fashioned kind of guy, you know." He let out a husky laugh.

"Rick, just last month you spent the night with my sister in a cabin. Are you trying to tell me that nothing happened that night? Yeah, right, try another one!" Sandra retorted in a sarcastic tone, stepping back to look at Amy again. Rick announced that he needed to go down to the stables to see if he figured out what was going on with Pride. He gave Amy a quick kiss and another slap on her behind.

"I will bring down some lunch," she answered his slap, pulling out a chair to sit down at the table at which Sandra again took her seat next to Philip, who went back to reading his paper.

Anna brought her over a plate of scrambled eggs with two slices of toast and a glass of juice. She wasn't sure if she would be able to stomach that and just pushed the plate forward and sipped on her juice.

"So…give me details, don't keep me waiting in suspense." She tapped the table with her hand, waiting patiently for her sister to spill the details of their wedding.

"Okay…here are some pictures from the wedding. I was totally surprised about it. I had the interview with Madeline Principal for the two days, and the third day I was feeling under the weather. Rick went out to get me some juice and crackers, and I had the epiphany that I hadn't had my period since December…"

At that point Philip got up, gave his wife a kiss on the forehead, and excused himself, explaining that it was time that he went off to work. Sandra just waved good-bye, still in awe over her sister's fantastic news. "So carry on, I think that we were getting a little too personal for Philip," she teased, looking at her sister, waiting for her to finish.

"Where was I? Oh, yeah, my period was long overdue, so I picked up a home pregnancy test, and we tested positive. I need to make an appointment today to see Dr. Gold to confirm." She broke for a moment to take another sip of her juice before she continued. "I was nervous as hell to tell Rick. After all, we never discussed having kids. The funny part of it all is that it never really dawned on either one of us that we hadn't been using any protection." She threw her head back as she let out a little laugh.

"So when did he ask you to marry him down there, I mean, I know that you are already engaged, but when did he say 'let's get married now'?" Sandi asked, still with enthusiasm and excitement. At this point, she had taken the pictures out of the envelope and started to look through them, ahhing and ohhing as she flipped through the photos. "Ames…what a beautiful wedding. You looked absolutely fabulous and so happy. What are we doing about the one planned for June?" she asked as she lifted her head to wait for the reply.

"Rick and I have decided that since we didn't have any family with us in Maui that we will still have the ceremony on June 20 as planned, but our anniversary will be March 26."

Down at the stables, Rick was having a difficult time believing that Tommy was using force to train Pride. Of everything that he had been reading on training for flat racing, it always said that they needed to be doing it gradually and with no violence toward the horse or they could retreat and not become trainable. But it was all falling into place, the subtle comments on his training practices from previous employers, Pride's attitude with running. From what he witnessed this morning, it was making sense. He had no other choice but to let Tommy go. He walked back to his office and took a seat and pulled out the résumé file to go through them again, thinking that they didn't have much time left to get someone here and train for the Kentucky Derby. He so wanted to be in that race this year. Maybe they should take a step back and get her ready by starting over, take it slow. He put his head in his hands and rested them on his desk, thinking.

Amy and Sandra had talked most of the morning away without realizing that it was almost lunchtime. She did manage to get a call into the doctor's office to set up an appointment with Dr. Gold the next day at nine thirty. She asked Anna to make some sandwiches and put some iced tea in the basket for her, that she would be right back down. Getting showered and dressed didn't take her long at all. She was looking forward to having lunch down at the stables. She was back in the kitchen within the half hour. Down at the stables, she left the lunch basket on his desk. Rick was nowhere to be seen. She looked in a number of places. His truck was still in the driveway. Where could he be? She waited another half hour then decided to go back to the house. He must have been really busy, and she didn't want to disturb him. She understood the problems that he was facing. If they couldn't get Pride to train right, then they wouldn't be able to qualify for the Kentucky Derby, something that he was looking forward to.

Back at the house, she played on her laptop in the family room, going online to look for house plans and designs. She needed something to keep her mind occupied. Rick didn't have the time to be training her on the ins and outs of running a successful breeding and racing ranch and trying to get Pride ready. She found a few that she really liked. She knew that Rick really only wanted a bungalow, and she could live with that. Their original plan was a small two-bedroom, but she was thinking more long-term now they had a family to think of. How many children did he want? Suppose they could start with a nice three-bedroom, ranch-style, say twenty-five hundred square feet? The kids' bedrooms on one side and the master with an en suite on the other side of the house?

She decided to go into town to the hardware store where they sold home-design plans. Something that she could look through and then show to Rick. Yeah, that was a good plan. She hopped into her car and drove into town. She parked at the town square. Shopping would help ease her mind. She could not remember the last time that she had so much time on her hands. Was she really getting restless? Sophie had managed through the years to keep her busy doing something. She was always jaunting here or there. This was so different. Maybe she should consider taking some courses, business, home decorating, or even home cooking. They were going to have a home of their own, so she couldn't rely on Anna to come down and cook for them all the time. She had a job to do at the main house. Cooking was definitely a good idea. She didn't mind the odd meal that she managed to muster up before at her condo.

She stopped off at the local college to get a class schedule. This would give her some insight on the courses, et cetera. Talking to the school's counselor about the cooking classes that they offered, she decided that this was not something that she wanted to get into. Better plan, contact Susie and see if she was still looking for work, offer her a job here to look after their new home. Now she was on a roll, next to the hardware store, browsing around at the appliances and dishware first, and then she asked the clerk for some help in finding the design-plan catalogs that they carried. After telling them that they were only interested in ranch-style homes, they helped her pick out the right one. She thanked them and asked for some builders' names that they could recommend. They provided her with a list of about five contractors with phone numbers.

From there she went window shopping. There was no sense in actually buying any new outfits yet, since she didn't know what would fit come a couple of months down the road. She glanced at her watch. It was almost dinnertime. *Better head back to the ranch.*

Dinner was rather quiet that night. Rick didn't come up from the stables, either. When she questioned Sandra if she had talked to him, her reply was that he would be working late and not to wait up for him. That was a little disappointing.

This went on almost a week and a half before Amy had had enough. She couldn't find him to tell him the good news that the doctor had confirmed her pregnancy. She saw her husband briefly at night when he crawled so tired into bed he barely had the strength to kiss her, and he was gone when she woke up in the morning. She almost felt like he had been avoiding her. Whenever she went down to the stables and could not find him, the guys would say that he was over there at Pride's stall or here at the office, but by the time that she got to where he was supposed to be he wasn't.

She had spent her days going through the design plans and keeping up her exercise regimen and eating way too much food. She heard that when a woman got pregnant she was eating for two, but she was beginning to feel that it was four or five that she was feeding. It didn't seem like it stopped. So the only way she knew was to keep herself as busy as possible swimming and exercising. She didn't outdo herself, and the doctor did provide her with examples of exercises that she could do that would not harm the baby.

Chapter Nineteen

Sandra and she went out one day to pick out baby furniture for her nursery and bought some baby clothes that they fell in love with. They had a ball shopping together. They didn't find anything at the local shops so they went into the city. Sandra indicated that she really liked the furniture that she saw online at IKEA, so they headed there first, and it turned out it was the only place that they needed. Amy didn't see anything that she really liked, plus she wasn't ready to start buying baby furniture yet. She wanted to have their home built first.

She had contacted a few of the contractors that the hardware store graciously provided for her, and they had set up a couple of meetings for early next week. She asked them for some references for her to check out in the meantime.

Rick was gone early again this morning. She was tired of chasing him down, and her ego was a little bruised. Since they had become a couple, this past week had been the longest that they had gone without being intimate. Maybe it was a test to make sure that they were compatible besides just in the bedroom. No, she would not go there. She knew that he loved her and she loved him. It was just a trying time of the year, especially since they all agreed to branch out into the thoroughbred racing.

Walking down the stairs to the family room, she called out to Sandi…"Sandi, Sandi, Sandi, where are you?" Listening for her to answer, she heard some rustling noises from the office. She walked in that direction…

"Sandi?" she called out as she got closer.

"Yeah, I'm in here, Ames…what's up?" She looked up from the desk.

"I had a thought upstairs…we have never discussed this, so I am just putting it out there…" She paused to gather her thoughts before she spoke again. "I think that now that he is a part of this family we should give Rick a promotion, kind of…" She took a seat in the chair directly in front of the desk.

"What are you talking about, give Rick a promotion? He runs the ranch. How much higher of a position can he get than that?" she quizzed her sister.

She was still shuffling papers as she continued to look for Andrew's birth certificate. Philip had told her that it was about time that she legally adopt Andrew. They had been married for almost five years now, and they never had done it. But he felt that it would help Andrew feel more secure once the baby arrives, and she totally agreed. She was in her own train of thought and only caught "share of the ranch." She shook her head and looked again at her sister and politely said, "Excuse me, what did you just say?"

"I can clearly see that you have something else on your mind. Perhaps this isn't the best time to bring it up…"

"No, I'm sorry…I have been looking for Andy's birth certificate all morning. Go ahead, please repeat it."

"I was saying that it was time that we made Rick a full partner of the ranch. With full authority to run the stables as he sees fit without having to come to us for every approval. Unless it's a huge expenditure. Then we all need to vote on it. What do you think?" Amy had been looking through the papers on the desk as well. She handed over to Sandi what she believed she had been looking for.

"Yes, that is it, thank you…Rick already has that kind of authority. Daddy gave that to him last year when Momma got sick. But you are right on the other part, that he should have his name on the deed to the ranch. Last year we added Philip's, so I only see it befitting. Have you talked to him about it yet? I can draw up the papers. I will have Alec pull the ones that were drawn up for Philip to sign and have them duplicated. One other matter that does sort of concern the ranch is did you guys have prenuptials drawn up? You personally have lots of money, and there is the Huckleberry ranch to consider and now Mystical," she concluded, taking the document and putting it into a folder then crossing her arms in front of her on the desk.

"No…We never had a prenuptial drawn up. It's not necessary, and I feel appalled that you are suggesting that anything will happen between us that we would need one!" she responded to her sister's comment. She was getting a little agitated by this conversation. As she stood up to leave before she said anything that she would regret, she added, "If you don't mind, just draw up the document that provides Rick with his share of the ranch entitlement, please." And on that note, she didn't look back, just strode out of the room in a huff.

She felt anger toward her sister for the first time since she met Hank and Daddy had tried to advise her not to marry him. How dare she suggest that they needed a prenuptial. *Does she have one with Philip? That was none of her business! The hell it wasn't, it would also concern the ranch.* That was the only income that Sandra would know. She certainly could afford the luxuries that Amy had. Well, maybe not quite as lavish, but they were far from hurting for cash. Daddy and Momma would have made sure of that, and she knew that once they turned thirty their inheritance would kick in. They both stood to inherit five million dollars each. They had already inherited the ranch and its operating capital. It was a business that was making money. Amy had seen the books.

Rick was doing interviews again today. So far he had not found anyone that he liked nor had Bob. At this rate he knew that they would not be ready for the Kentucky Derby. Their best bet was just enter Pride into the Triple Crown—the Canadian version of the Kentucky Derby. "We will start small and build her back up" is what he told Bob just this morning.

Terry Sanders was his next candidate. He was twenty, won a number of harness races at Kawartha Downs, won two seasons in a row, the Pepsi North at Woodbine, and with Lady Luck two years ago they won the Queen's Plate. It was quite impressive. He was due to arrive in ten minutes. Just enough time for him to go and grab a quick bite to eat from the mess hall.

As he walked up to the mess hall, Amy caught his eye. She always did. He could recognize her anywhere. She was getting into the car. He wondered where she was off to today. She hadn't been down to the stable in over a week. He wondered why and what he had done now to make her mad. She didn't stir at night when he crawled into bed beside her. In fact, she didn't even roll over when he tried to kiss her, or could he have been just so tired that he didn't feel her response? That had to be it. If she was mad at him, she would have said something long before now. It wasn't her style to keep it bottled up. He loved that about her, the way that she vented when she got angry. It was Friday afternoon. The weekend was approaching. He had to make note that he had to get up to the house in time for dinner tonight and spending some time with his bride. *Mental note to self—dinner is at six thirty—head up in time to shower and change. Surprise her.*

Terry was early. He didn't have time for that sandwich now, he had spent too much time watching his wife drive away and daydreaming of how it felt to have her in his arms that were aching to hold her. He gave his head a gentle shake to rid those thoughts for the time being. Back to work for now.

He introduced himself to Terry and directed him to the office, where they engaged in conversation. Terry was easy to talk to, and he didn't have any trouble talking about his accomplishments. He even brought with him copies of the cups that he had won and three glowing references.

"So tell me, Terry, why are you no longer working for Hickory Farms?" He asked the question although he already knew the answer.

The economy took its toll on a number of the stud farms in the area, and Hickory was unfortunately one of them. They had been selling off their stock for the past year. There was only one that he wished that he could have had, and that was Snowflake, but unfortunately, she came on the market the same time that Ivan had passed away, and there was no way that he was going to bring up a purchase that large at a time like that. Terry, ending his response, jerked him back to the present.

"I am really impressed with your résumé, Terry. I truly think that you would be a great asset to Mystical. When do you think that you can start?" He reached for the young lad's hand to shake.

"Sir…Thank you. I am looking forward to a great career here. I can be here on Monday, seven a.m. sharp, sir." He took Rick's hand and they shook.

"Why don't I take you around, introduce you to Bob, he's our training and breeding manager, and to some of the other guys and gals that you will be working with. And mostly to Pride. She will be your baby. We want to take her to the Kentucky Derby, and I think that you are the guy to help us do that," he said with a smile and then walked him out into the stables. First he walked him over to Pride's stall and introduced them. To his amazement, it was like Pride had known him. Terry was in love with Pride, and after a few minutes to let them continue with their love affair, he took him down a ways to Bob. They talked for a half an hour and confirmed the time that Terry should be there on Monday.

It was only three o'clock in the afternoon. He still had paperwork to fill out and feed orders to process, and the mess hall needed supplies, or so Tammy was telling him just this morning. He went back to his office and closed the door so that he wouldn't be disturbed.

Amy had gone into the city to cool down, and this time she went to a country-and-western store and purchased a pair of cowboy boots, a lady Stetson, and a pair of chaps. It was about time that she started to act the part of a ranch owner. She might as well look the part. Next she went into the department store and found a bright-white T-shirt. She tried on a size smaller than she would normally have bought for herself, but she had a motive, and if she wanted her plan to work, it was time to call in her marker. One of her fantasies since meeting Rick was about to come to life. She wanted her man back, and what better way than to seduce him in his own element.

She arrived back home in time to get changed, and since what she was wearing was not really suitable for prancing through the house, she grabbed her father's overcoat from the hall closet and then headed for the stables. With any luck she would be missing out on dinner, too, tonight. Passing through the kitchen she ran into Anna, who looked at her strangely, but hey, the girls were always doing strange things. She asked her not to set a place for her tonight, that she had plans to take Rick out for dinner if she could pry him away from the ranch long enough.

Amy peered into the office window to see him leaning back in his chair, feet up on the desk and his arms across his chest. A second look. She couldn't see his face. It was covered by his Stetson…Ah, her baby was grabbing a nap. *Quick note to self…this will revitalize him in ways that he never thought of.*

She quietly opened the door and just as softly closed and locked it. Next she pulled the blinds down, her back to him, and his voice startled her…"I know that you are here. I told you before you are my sixth sense…"

She quickly turned on her heels. He had not moved a muscle yet. She turned on the CD player that she brought down with her. It was low and soft music, just something to set her mood. He shifted in his seat to take a peek at what she was up to just as she dropped her overcoat and climbed onto the desk…

"*Wow*, baby!" His feet flew off the desk, and he pushed his chair back to admire the view…What was she doing? She was dancing with her hips swaying to the music. He took another look at his bride. She just had on chaps and cowboy boots. He looked further up her magnificent body, she revealed a tight-fitting, white T-shirt, no bra. The T-shirt hugged her firm tits, and her nipples were taut and begging for attention. Hips still moving to the rhythm of the music, her hands now came up and squeezed her tits together. Watching her gave him an instant erection. She was wearing a Stetson of her own…

"*Wow*, Momma!" he squealed and rolled his chair closer to the desk. Her long, firm, lean legs were spread apart. It gave him a nice view of her crotch. He licked his lips, and she watched him as she lifted her top slowly, seductively, up over her breasts, teasing, revealing glimpses of one boob at a time, then finally up over her head the hat went flying to the floor with the shirt close behind it. She wiggled down to a squatting position on the desk, jutting her chest out to him. He went to reach out to her, and she shook her head.

"No, no, no." But she was not fast enough as he grabbed her legs and pulled her down onto her butt on the desk, her feet resting on his chair. Just as quickly he had his arms wrapped around her still-tiny waist, pulling himself closer to her as he planted a hungry kiss on her hot, waiting mouth that was just as hungry for his kiss. Their tongues found each other and did a dance all their own. His hands roamed and rubbed her backside for a few moments before they found their way to the front, massaging her firm tits. She let out a soft moan of pleasure as his fingers played with her nipples, pulling and pinching them, and she squirmed under his touch.

He started to trace her neckline with kisses and licks, nibbling on her ear then down to her areola where he licked around and around, sending shivers of pure desire through her. She cried out his name, and he moaned as he squeezed her tit and took its nipple into his mouth, suckling and pulling on it with his teeth. He felt his cock grow rock hard against his jeans, but she wasn't ready yet for that. Placing one hand on her back and the other on her abdomen, he gently pushed her back, removing his hands so that he could lift her legs and feet to rest them on the desk. He wanted a better view of her feminine folds, the beautiful, well-manicured, auburn curls.

He could feel the heat that was generated from her as his face got closer. He rubbed his nose up against her clit, and he looked up into her face. She was resting on her elbows and watching his every move. His finger ran along the inside of her thigh, and her moans were getting a little louder. She reached for the boom box to turn it up just a little louder, and he had to smile to himself. She was being self-conscious about their lovemaking noises. Moving his fingers to her crotch, he rubbed them up and down along her folds, stopping the second time at her center. His tongue was now dancing around her clit, and her hips were dancing in tune to his tongue. He slipped not one but two fingers into her center, and she let out several husky cries of pleasure as she climaxed for him, tasting oh-so-sweet. She was ready. He removed his fingers and pushed his chair back as he stood.

She hungrily reached forward and grabbed him by his jeans, fumbling with the belt and button, cursing under her breath with little panting breaths. Finally they were undone, and she pulled them down as far as she could reach. He didn't waste a moment as he grabbed her by the legs, pulling so that she was on the edge of the desk as he slammed his rock-hard cock deep inside her. He pumped in and out. He had a rhythm going in tune with the music. Harder, deeper. She moaned as she reached and grabbed onto his ass, digging her nails into his cheeks. She anxiously reached to take off his T-shirt. Lifting it up over his head, she hungrily reached up to nip at his nipples, sending waves of pleasure through him.

"Baby…I'm coming…Ready or not, here's Daddy…" he moaned into her ear, one more deep thrust stopping there, and he felt her thighs tighten in contraction to hold on to him. He felt the wave of warmth fill them both. She sighed as she let go and let her top half flop back onto the desk.

Slightly supporting herself on her elbows again, she looked deep into his eyes, whispering, "How did you enjoy that fantasy?" and reaching with one hand to run her fingers down his hairy chest. He was still inside her. He was rock hard again…

"Baby, you can come down here anytime you want to distract me! Are you ready for round two?" Looking into her smiling face, he had the answer that he was looking for. She was ready. This time, without missing a beat, he wrapped her legs around him as he picked her up and walked over to the wall where he pushed her up against it, taking her arms and placing them above her head as he held her there, pumping her like a jackrabbit on an oil field, pumping and pumping and waiting for the gusher to come. It didn't take as long this time around. Still holding her there, he placed another hungry kiss on her swollen lips. She let her legs go from around him, and he slid from inside her, letting her slowly slide down the wall.

He stood before her shirtless, and his near-perfect six-pack abs, his firm pecs all felt great under her touch. She kept sliding down until her mouth was at his cock level. She took it into her hand. It was still warm and slightly sticky, and before he could say another word, she had him in her mouth, up and down his shaft, suckling, licking. He moaned as he placed his hand at the back of her head to help in her movement. He jerked forward, pushing his cock deeper into her mouth, and she moaned and slurped…Moments later, he came in her mouth. She liked the taste of him. He had had sweets today and a burger. She could taste the spice that the mess hall cook used on her burgers. She finished and rose to meet him.

"I'm really happy that I decided to come down here tonight…" she said as she wrapped her arms around him, realizing that his jeans were still around his ankles. She let out a little giggle.

"What is so amusing? I am glad that you decided to come down here tonight, too! What a fantastic way to start a weekend." He released her just long enough to pull up his pants. In doing so, he commented, "That's one hell of a costume you have there, Mrs. Durham." Smirking at her as he reached a little farther over for her T-shirt, he picked it up and helped her with putting it back on. Just then, there was a knock on the door. It was Bob calling to him. He then hurriedly grabbed her coat and motioned for her to go and sit in his chair. She quickly did as he asked as he did up his pants and went to the door, unlocking it to open.

"Hey, what's up? The Mrs. and I were just going over the work schedule for the weekend. I won't be coming down until Monday morning." His tone suggested that it was a statement rather than a comment.

Bob was eying the office. There were a few papers on the floor. What business was it of his if his boss wanted to frump his wife in his office? He took note that his boss was shirtless. He chuckled to himself. "I just wanted to let you know my opinion of Terry. Did you have a minute to go over his résumé with me, or is this a bad time?" He gave his boss a grin that told him that he really knew what went on behind the closed door. Feeling her face flush a little, squirming in her seat, she found amusement in the man's banter. Rick turned to look at her, asking with his eyes if she was all right there…She jumped into the conversation.

"It's all right, Bob. I think that we have the schedule just about wrapped up, thanks for asking. I appreciate everything that you can do to help lighten Rick's workload. I have not seen much of him since we returned from Maui." She looked at her husband adoringly. He now took residence in the chair in front of the desk.

He half crossed his leg over the other. Catching the Stetsons still on the floor off to the side of the desk along with his shirt, he quickly looked back to Bob.

"So what do you want to know about Terry? Didn't you talk to him earlier?" He turned for just a fraction to reach for Terry's résumé. It was, ah, right there. He picked it up…Ehh, it had a boot print on it. He could explain if necessary…He handed it to Bob, who in turn read it along with Rick's scribbled notes.

"Very impressive for a twenty-year-old. What about his references? Have you talked to any of them yet?" He looked at his boss. He trusted Rick's judgment, and he liked the kid.

"Look, Bob, why don't I come back down tomorrow morning before lunch, and we can discuss this some more, but for right now I know that Amy here is anxiously waiting for dinner. I detained her long enough, and I'm kind of famished myself. How does that sound?" He turned again to look at Amy as she sat there patiently, only half-dressed.

"Sure, I will let you two go for dinner. Enjoy dessert, too!" He winked at Rick, letting him know that he really knew what happened behind closed doors, but he wasn't about to tell anyone.

They finally made it back to the comfort of their room for the night. They flopped down on their bed, laughing together.

"Hey, did I tell you how much I love you lately? Or how sexy you looked in that outfit tonight?" He rolled over to his side to look into her caring eyes.

"Let me see, when was the last time I heard those words? I believe it was this morning as you closed the bedroom door. You probably thought that I wasn't awake. Surprise!" She rolled on top of him and poked him in the ribs. "I have been awake every morning when you get up and leave. Please don't do that anymore…Wake me if I am sleeping. I promise that I will try not to be grouchy or get mad. I would like us to start each day off right with at least a kiss and 'I love you.'" She smiled at him as she ran her hand up under his T-shirt and massaged his chest. He agreed that they should start each day in just that manner and even suggested a little foreplay or nookie. She just giggled and said, "We'll see." With that, they snuggled into bed for the night.

Chapter Twenty

End of May

Invitations for their wedding started to come back. She was getting excited to finally meet his family. They had talked several times on the phone to his mom out in British Columbia. They joined Facebook to chat with his brothers and sister. Everyone now knew that they had already gotten married in Maui in March. She talked every week with Trish, Rick's sister, on Facebook. She was looking forward to them coming in June.

They decided to cancel the officiant and skip the ceremony and just to have a big reception party instead, and they invited a few more friends to the celebration. Her nerves were getting frayed with the plans for the reception and finally getting the building permits to start the process on their new home, which they were hoping to have done by the time that the baby arrived in late September. It was a give-or-take couple of days. Everything was going well. Sandra passed her bar exam and had interviews with several prestigious law firms in the city that were looking promising for her. Her pregnancy had been showing for a few months now, which scared her a little more. Philip told her that she didn't have to go out and get a job right away, that it didn't even make sense to him with her due date approaching so fast that she would just find a job and have to leave to have the baby. During Sandra's last ultrasound, they found out the sex of their baby but were keeping it a secret from the others. Rick and Amy decided that they didn't want to know the sex of their bundle of joy. All they wanted was a healthy baby.

There was a knock on the study door. It interrupted her thoughts.

"Come in," she called out from behind the desk.

"Miss Amy. There is a gentleman here to see you. He said that it is urgent," Anna announced as she opened the office door.

"This man, where is he now, Anna?" she asked as she stood.

"In the living room, Miss," Anna replied.

"Okay. Thank you, Anna." She came out from behind the desk and proceeded to the living room to greet her guest. She had no idea who he was or what he wanted, only that it was of urgent nature.

Upon entering the living room, she noticed the man standing next to the fireplace. He was dressed in an expensive Italian suit. His grayish hair indicated that he was an older gentleman.

"Hello, can I help you, sir? I am Amy Gordon-Durham. I was told that you needed to see me, that it was of an urgent matter?" she said as she approached the gentleman and extended her hand.

"Hello, Miss Gordon. Your photos do not do you any justice. You are much more beautiful in person. I apologize for the intrusion, but my client is in need of your help. Sorry, let me introduce myself, my name is Avril Lyons—attorney at law," he replied as he shook her hand.

"I am sorry, but I don't understand the nature of your visit. Please have a seat." She gestured for him to sit in the wing chair to her right as she sat on the opposite side.

"My client is up on attempted-murder charges of a Jack Hayes. I received your name from a complaint that you filed last year with your local police. If I understand it correctly, Mr. Hayes took several nude photographs of you along with a videotape. Is that correct?" he asked as he took out a notebook from his briefcase.

"Yes, that is correct. But I still fail to see what I can do to help your client, as I did not file charges against Mr. Hayes."

"I believe that you could be a character witness for my client."

"Mr. Lyons, I'm not sure that I can do that. I have a reputation to protect, not only my own, but my business here at the ranch. Can I ask who is your client?"

"I understand completely. I believe you know her as Indigo. Her real name is Lucy Lambert," he replied as he looked up from his notes.

"Yes, I know Indigo, but what is the connection with Mr. Hayes?" She was trying to piece this all together to make some sense from it all.

"Mr. Hayes took some incriminating photos of Ms. Lambert and tried to extort money from her. She filed charges against him. When he was served a restraining order I guess he lost control and came after her one night after he had been drinking heavily. In an attempt to protect herself, she came at him with all her might. I really can't give you more details than that right now. What do you say? Will you help her?" he asked in a soft, caring tone that she believed was genuine, not just some gimmick to get her to help.

"Let me talk it over with my husband and I will get back to you. When do you need my answer, Mr. Lyons?" she asked as she stood, more or less indicating that the conversation was over.

Mr. Lyons stood then, too, before he responded. "As soon as you can get back to me, it would be appreciated. Here, please take my card, it has all the numbers where you can reach me." Handing her his card, he put his notebook away.

"Like I said, I will need to discuss with my husband first. But I will give it careful consideration. Let me show you the way out." She started toward the front door, showing the man out. She waited for him to start his car and head back down the driveway before she closed the door.

Careful consideration she would give it. Indigo was a coworker, they shared the same agent—Sophie. They worked together a couple of times. But she always thought of her to be a little "flighty." On the other hand, no one deserved that kind of treatment for humiliation.

She was confident that Rick would want her to do the right thing, and that was to help Indigo.

The family all came to the agreement that they would hold off on entering in the Kentucky Derby this year, with the setbacks that they took in their training with Pride. But now things were progressing rather nicely, Terry was doing an excellent job with Pride, and they were ready for the Queen's Plate race—the first in the Triple Crown series—in June, and everyone was looking forward to that.

Terry had her doing one minute and fifty-three seconds. From everything that Rick had been reading on the oval tracks and thoroughbred racing, the best time ever was in 2004 by Starlight, who won the race in one minute and forty-nine seconds. So by his calculations they still had more training to do to get her time perfected. Terry had rapidly become a great asset to the ranch, and Rick was very proud of the accomplishments that he was making with Pride and working well with the other ranch hands.

Rick was getting nervous. He hadn't seen his family in over five years. Sure, he talked to them lots on the phone, but he just never took the time after his first wife passed away to go and visit. So to have them all here was going to be great. They had made arrangements with the local hotel to have rooms reserved for their guests, and Amy insisted they at least have his mother stay with them in the other guest room.

The basement and foundation walls had been poured a couple of days ago, and today the framing of the house was taking place. After several long conversations, they finally agreed to build a four-bedroom home. It was much bigger than Rick really wanted, but, hey, this was what kept her happy. They chose the Mediterranean Colonnade design, rounding in at thirty-seven hundred square feet in size, with a two-car garage, and they would provide a suite above the garage for Susie to live in, since she agreed to come work for them once the house was built.

The crew that they hired was doing a fabulous job so far with the house. They were keeping in or under budget, which she loved. Amy had been known to be a little frugal at times, but she knew that her budget for the building and design of the house had to stay in the five hundred thousand range. She was not going to spend more than that, and according to her research, what she set aside should be more than plenty to build their dream home.

They were in bed reading when Amy broke the comfortable silence between them.

"Honey, I forgot to tell you the other day that I had a visitor come to the house. A lawyer. It seems that our friend Mr. Hayes has gotten himself into a nice mess this time around. He tried to blackmail a friend. She has been charged with attempted murder," she said as she laid her book down on her nightstand and then turned to look at her adoring husband while she awaited his response.

"Oh really? Too bad she didn't follow through with it. I'm sorry, that was totally uncalled for. So what did this lawyer want, exactly?" he asked as he now turned his attention to her.

"He wants me to be a character witness for her. And he would like an answer as soon as possible. I told him that I needed to discuss it with you first."

"I trust your decisions, Ames. You do whatever it is that you need to do, as long as you don't get hurt in the process. That includes not getting stressed out, we don't want anything to hurt our little bundle you are carrying." He spoke softly to her as he gently rubbed her belly.

"All right, I promise to be careful. I think that I need to do this, for closure. I can't see this slime getting away with another attempt. Enough talk about him for the night. I'm tired. I love you, good night." With that she leaned over to give him a kiss good night.

"Good night, sweetheart. I love you, too!"

She called Mr. Lyons in the morning to tell him that she would help out Indigo. He thanked her and said he would be in touch again to arrange a meeting.

It was two days before the celebration. His mother was due to arrive just after lunch. Around eleven, she called the limo service to come and pick them up so that they could be at the airport in time to greet her. They arrived at the terminal just as her plane landed. Rick nervously held her hand. His palm was sweaty. She gave his arm a quick little jerk to get his attention.

Looking up into his eyes that were somewhat hidden by his Stetson, she said, "Hon, it's okay. I don't understand why you are so jittery." Then she placed a sweet little kiss on his lips. He did return her kiss but kept his eyes on the gate as passengers were starting to exit.

"You don't understand. It's been almost five years since I have seen her. I didn't even go home when Leanne passed away." He looked down at his adoring wife but still kept an eye out for his mother. He pointed and said, "Look, there she is…Mom…Alison Durham." He called out to her, letting go of Amy's hand to walk toward his mother. They embraced for a long time, and it touched Amy's heart knowing that he missed his family, but with everything that had gone on they were not a close family, either. His mother was taller than average. She looked about fifty years young. She had brown hair with blonde streaks, olive skin tones, and she still looked very fit. Her eyes were those that one could read every caring feeling she possessed with a hint of gray in a shade of green, and her jaw line was square with a petite, straight nose.

"Mom, I would like to introduce you to the love of my life…Amy Gordon Durham. Ames, this is my mother, Alison Durham." Taking a stand beside his wife, he waited for his mother to comment.

"Amy, dear, it is a pleasure to finally meet you, your voice on the phone does not do your beauty justice. I see that there is something that the two have of you have seemed to have left out." She took her new daughter-in-law into an embrace, rubbing Amy's protruding stomach, which now felt like it was bulging. Amy felt huge, although Rick said she was not huge.

"The pleasure is all mine, Mrs. Durham. We thought that it was best that we waited until everyone was together before we announced our little surprise. We couldn't be happier that you have come to join us." She gave the woman a firm hug.

"Well, when is the bundle of joy expected to make its appearance? And, dear, please call me Mom." She took her by the waist to leave the area and claim her luggage. "Rick dear, here is my claim ticket. Why don't you go and get my suitcases while Amy and I chat and walk to the car?" She headed Amy toward the exit, leaving Rick behind. Amy could feel his loving stare as the two women left him.

"Our bundle is due around the end of September. We are really excited, and, no, the baby is not why we got married, just to ease your mind. I love your son. He is the most important person in my life, next to our unborn child. Rick proposed to me before we knew that I was pregnant. We found out about it while we were in Hawaii in March. That is when we decided to step up the wedding. We had a beautiful ceremony in Maui. Your son arranged it all. I have pictures to show you once we get to the ranch." They arrived at the waiting limo. Alison was impressed with the ride. A few steps behind them was Rick, and then they all climbed into the limo.

The women chatted more in the car, and Rick just sat there listening to them gab and discuss names for the baby. A few they liked and others they didn't. They were not going to decide on one now. It was too early. Amy learned that this was the first time since Trisha, Rick's sister, moved to Australia six years ago that the family had been together. That gave her a happy feeling that she had a hand in bringing his family home." Mom, did Amy tell you that she has an identical twin sister?" he asked, sitting across from her, looking at his wife adoringly.

"No, she didn't. What is that like, especially with you all living under one roof? I hope that you don't play awful tricks that twins seem to play in movies," Alison said with a hint of humor in her voice while looking at Amy with a smile on her face.

"They certainly do. It's horrible, Mom…As it turns out, her sister is also pregnant. We had to do a paternity test just to make sure that we had the respective wives." Rick burst into laughter, slapping his leg at his attempt of humor. By the expression on Alison's face, she didn't find it humorous at all.

"Rick, that's not funny at all. Apologize now to your Mom. Alison, we don't play those games anymore. Besides, we don't look like identical twins anymore. You will see that my sister has this really casual look, her hair is much shorter than mine, and she is further along in her pregnancy than I." She reached to slap Rick's lap and take his hand.

"Mom, I am sorry. That wasn't funny at all. I would know my wife anywhere. She's my sixth sense. I just thought I would put a little humor in. Obviously it was in poor taste." He gave her a little-boy frown. He held his wife's hand and gave her his adoring smile.

"I picked up on the humor, son. I see that you two are much in love, that is a wonderful thing. I remember your father and our life. He did the best that he could. God bless his soul. He would be very proud of each of his kids." A tear trickled down her cheek. Rick reached to wipe it away with his thumb and squeezed in between the two women to embrace his mother. She let out a few sobs and continued, "I'm okay. This is a happy time for you. I don't want to spoil your celebration."

"You are not spoiling anything, Mom. I am just so happy that you are here with us. We want you to know that you are welcome to stay as long as you like or come back whenever you want." She reached across Rick to take her hand into hers. The rest of the ride was quiet with tidbits of conversation. Rick had mentioned that they were entering Pride into the Triple Crown this year, and the first race was next weekend. He talked with pride and ownership in the ranch.

Giving him a share in the ranch was her wedding present to him, and she was planning to give it to him at the reception.

The next couple of days were a whirlwind, people coming and going, getting the gazebos set up for the reception, the dance floor. She must have been online a number of times that day to make sure that the weather was going to hold out.

Josh, Rick's eldest brother, and his wife Rebecca, arrived yesterday morning at the hotel, as did Peter, the middle brother, and his girlfriend Denise. And just in time for dinner at the restaurant, Trisha came waltzing in. Amy found that she was drawn in by this gorgeous bombshell. She was tall, lean, with legs that didn't seem to end, the most beautiful blonde, wavy hair, and as she got closer she saw her mother's eyes, a hint of gray to green. She saw the resemblance in all the boys, but Trisha, she was a much-younger version of their mother. They had a fabulous time at dinner. She sat back and watched them all several times as they laughed about their younger days and they reminisced about their father. She saw the pride and adoration that each of his children held for the man. Josh and Peter teased Rick to no end for his love of horses when he piped in, "I may not have a 'man's' job, according to two fools, but I know my horses, and I have one the world's best-looking palominos sitting here at this table." He turned to look at his wife, as if he saw her for the first time again.

"You always were a sap, Rick!" Trish reached across the table to slap his arm. "So why don't you tell us more about the wedding in Maui? Why the change in venue?" she continued.

It was Rick who answered his sister. "I've never really been anywhere in this world, I mean I never really traveled, and when Ames was busy in Maui doing her interview with Ms. Principal, well, I had the opportunity to visit the island, and I fell in love with it, almost as much as I love this woman sitting beside me. I just knew that it was the right time and place to pledge my life to her." Before he continued, he looked into her eyes, as if to ask for permission to tell the rest of the family. She wore a loose-fitting dress, so it was not obvious to the naked eye. She nodded her approval, placing her hand on her belly. "I had already made all the arrangements to surprise her when she gave me a little surprise of her own. She told me that we were pregnant, and that is when I knew I had made the right decision. So that is why we didn't wait."

Josh was the first one to rise from the table with his glass to toast his baby brother and his new bride. "To you, little bro. And to Amy for putting up with all your stink. Congratulations to you both. May you both live a long and happy life together filled with many more babies." He raised his glass and everyone said, "Here here, congratulations to the happy couple."

It was truly a happy occasion. The dinner was stupendous, and his family was awesome. One felt their love, generosity, and sincerity right in this room. They may not have lived close by each other in the last decade, but that did not separate their bond. Amy was proud to be accepted into this family. The girls talked about the reception tomorrow, their careers. Amy didn't brag about her career or the places that she had been, it was just casual, good conversation, the odd time she would mention someone famous that she partied with. The other ladies thought she had this glamorous life and asked questions as to what they were like to be around, just the usual questions one would ask about a celebrity. No one was out to impress anyone that night. Rick had remembered that Peter always wanted to become a real estate tycoon like Larry Krump when he thought he would throw him a bone. "Hey Pete…you ever get your realtor's license?"

"Yeah. Why, you looking for prime land to purchase to stow away your bride?" He laughed.

"No, I just thought I would introduce you to someone that could be beneficial to your career tomorrow…Larry Krump is going to be at the reception."

He grinned at Amy, who slapped his arm and said, "You are bad."

"Okay, bro…You're not serious about the Krump being at your reception?" Peter asked, looking at his brother then to Amy for an answer, not sure if they were pulling his leg or not. But judging from the conversations that they had been having all evening and the circle that Amy traveled in, he was not one hundred percent sure.

Amy nodded her head as if to agree with her husband, then verbally confirmed.

"No way! How do you know the Krump, man?" Peter asked, now looking at his girlfriend in total awe. He was being given the opportunity to meet one of his idols.

"Larry and I go back to wife number two, Marla. Marla and I shared the same agent. Then I bought my condo from Larry. He has been one of my closest, dearest friends. I would love for you all to meet him and Lonnie, his current wife, in case you weren't sure," Amy announced. And on that note, Amy wanted to change the subject. She never was comfortable talking about herself or her career. To her, it always felt like bragging about the people that she knew and how much money one had to have to rub elbows with the elite society. Turning to Trisha, she asked, "So what type of work do you do in Australia?"

"I travel with the Formula One racers. I interview the drivers and pit crews. I am really enjoying it. I love the thrill of the race, the speed, all of it," Trisha answered, then continued, "and since you all are here, no better than the present to let you all know that I have also taken back our last name…" Silence filled the small banquet room. Her brothers all stared at her, shaking their heads in disbelief.

Josh spoke. "Are you nuts, Trish? Everything that Dad worked so hard for, and you want to risk it all. You just admitted that you have your face plastered on the TV, and I am sure in magazines as well.

What if Sontiago recognizes you? Have you ever thought about that?" Before he could say another word, Alison jumped in to her daughter's defense.

"Guys…Before you go condemning your sister, don't you think that you owe it to her to find out why she did this?" She pushed her chair back to get up and go to her daughter's side.

"Thank you, Mom. I am not stupid, despite what you think, Josh. I am not this dumb blonde that only thinks of herself. I did my research. I talked to the FBI before I made my decision. And they agreed with me. My life is not in danger and nor is anyone else's at this table. The vendetta is over. We can lead long, happy lives. I am proud of things that Dad accomplished and the things that he did to protect his family. But I am also proud of my real last name, Andrews, and I don't want my life to be a lie anymore. I also talked it over with Mom…" Turning to look at their mother, she found the strength to continue. "She supports my decision. Besides, Andrews is a popular last name. I have to believe that if I stay out of Sontiago's way, our paths will never cross. So whether you like it or not, too bad, and suck it up!" The smirk on her face told them that she was quite capable of looking after herself.

Rick got up and went over to his sister. "I am proud of you, sis. I think that it is high time that we all took what was ours back. I, too, have been talking to the FBI. Amy's life is an open book. She is constantly in the media. I had to make sure that everything was okay with them before I told her the truth about our family. We had a little scare of our own when we were in Maui…" He continued to tell them about the incident and that the FBI confirmed that they had their lives back.

Chapter Twenty-One

It was well after nine o'clock that night when everyone left the restaurant, pleased and happy. Momma Alison was staying at the ranch with them, and the others had a room across the street. Amy gave each brother a hug and a kiss good night and thanked them again for coming out to help them celebrate their union.

Once back at the ranch, Rick slipped down to the stables to check on a couple of things that needed attending. He said good night to his mom and kissed Amy and promised that he wouldn't be down there very long and asked her to wait up for him.

Back up at the house, Alison turned to Amy, as she had already started up the stairs to the guest room. "Amy, dear, if you don't mind me asking, what are your plans now that you are with child and married to my son?"

"Alison…My intentions?" She paused at the bottom of the stairs and looked up at her mother-in-law, thinking that it was a strange question, but also respecting her enough to respond. "My intentions, I assure you, are honourable. I truly found my soul mate in Rick. I would lay my life on the line for him and our child. As for my career, I really do not know. We have discussed it, and I am willing to give it all up to be with him and our family. I have already told my agent that I want to give it up." Tears started to well up in her eyes. This was something that she wished that she had shared with her own mother. She continued. "Financially, your son will not want for anything. I want to stand beside him and help him realize his own dreams as well as my own father's and turn this ranch into the best that it can be." At that point she did not hear Rick come back into the house. All she felt was his arm wrap around her waist and his lips on the top of her head.

"Thank you, Amy. I appreciate your honesty, and I can tell that you two were meant to be. I will leave you two for the night and see you in the morning. I love you both," Alison said and blew them both a kiss good night as she climbed the stairs.

Rick twirled her around so that she was facing him. Holding her and looking into her tearstained eyes, he first wiped her cheeks, placing a soft kiss on each side before he spoke. "You survived the Andrews clan. I am impressed. I am truly impressed with your comments to satisfy my mother. I love you and our family and would lay down my life as well. But don't you think that if we both laid down our lives for one another our children would be parentless?" He added a note of teasing to his voice. She playfully slapped his chest. They walked together upstairs to their room for the night. The rest of the house was quiet. Everyone had turned in for the night. Tomorrow was a big day. Their festivities were scheduled to start around three in the afternoon.

The morning was really busy for the women as they all had dates at the spa, and then it was off to the hairdressers. The men had decided to go out for a ride on the ranch.

Rick was excited to show his brothers this amazing piece of property. He loved it as if it were his own. The guys had an awesome time out riding around, and Rick stopped by the office one last time before they all headed up to the house to get ready.

Amy had left his clothes out on the bed for him. He came into the room to find her sitting in the chair with her feet up on the bed, not even dressed yet.

"Is everything okay, sweetie?" he asked as he bent down to give her a kiss.

"Yep, just a little tired. This morning's activities took a lot more out of me than I thought that they would. Sandra is taking a nap as well." She looked up at him with a passion that stirred deep in her soul. She meant everything that she had told Alison last night, Rick was her soul mate. She loved him with all her being.

"Are you going to be okay today, baby? Is there anything that I can do to help out? Come over here and sit with me. I need to hold you." As he sat on their bed, she got up and sat on his lap and wrapped her arms around him as she spoke. "Joe and Anna have everything under control downstairs…" Letting go for just a moment to get the papers from her dresser, she came back over and sat back down on his lap, handing them to him.

He looked puzzled. "What is this?" he asked as he took the envelope and opened it up to pull the paper out. He read the document, and total surprise overcame his face. He looked at her. "Are you sure that you want to do this? I mean. I don't know what I mean. You know that I love this place, but it's yours and Sandra's."

"Honey, I talked it over with Sandra and Philip. Daddy gave Philip a share in the ranch just after he married Sandra. We all agreed that you have done an awesome job with it so far, and it was the only thing to do. It is only right that you have a share in this, too. Helping you realize your dreams is what I want to do. Together, let's build this ranch into the best thoroughbred racing ranch." She embraced him again. He placed a hungry kiss against her anxiously waiting mouth. Their kiss was getting them both worked up. It was hot and heavy when she gently pushed him away. "It's time that we start getting ready to meet our guests. We can pick this up later tonight." She smiled at him as she left his lap to get dressed.

"Okay, boss lady, if you say so, but I am holding you to the rain check." He laughed as he started to strip to head into the shower, and he rubbed his naked body up against her half-naked body. She felt his warmth and his semierection, and just as he was passing her, she couldn't help herself. She reached out and slapped his bare ass. He quickly turned his head and winked at her before he climbed into the shower to get ready. By the time that he came out she was gone. He continued to get ready to meet her downstairs. They agreed to meet their guests together.

Downstairs, Amy was seeing to the final touches. Her last surprise arrived. J.J. Strait was their special guest. She met him a couple of years ago on one of her assignments in Nashville, and they had become good friends. And when she called him to tell him that she had met her soul mate and they were getting married, he offered to come and play at her wedding.

"J.J. Thank you so much for coming. Rick is going to be so tickled when he meets you. He enjoys your music so much. We both do. You know that already." She was giving him a hug when Rick came downstairs. He didn't recognize him from the back, all he saw was the Stetson and his wife hugging him. His rage of jealousy overcame him until he saw her eyes light up over the man's shoulder. She patted J.J.'s back and let go.

"Rick, honey…My last surprise for you is here. Please come over here. I would like to introduce you to…" Before she could get the words out, J.J. had turned around, and the expression on Rick's face was priceless.

"J.J. Strait! Pleasure to meet you, sir." He extended his hand as he reached the pair of them standing at the family room doorway. He beamed at his wife. It was a great surprise, and he had to wonder how many more of these little surprises he had coming. The men shook hands and struck up a conversation about breeding thoroughbreds. Rick would never have guessed that he would be talking with celebrities of this caliber. She left the two gentlemen to help Anna and Sandra with a few last-minute details outside. Moments later, the two came outside, and Rick showed him the area that they had set up for the band. J.J. left briefly to get the rest of his band and set up.

Things were running smoothly, and guests were starting to arrive. Amy was having the time of her life, laughing and talking with everyone as they walked around, making their rounds. J.J. had set up and was playing in the background. People were talking and appeared to be having a good time. As she promised Peter, she'd introduced him to Larry Krump, who was a sport about it all, and as a special favour to her he agreed to share a few real estate tips with her new brother-in-law. She left the two men to chat as she continued to make her rounds. Sophie was here, Tori Mahaffey and Sean McDermott came, and Brooke Fields and her hubby arrived. She introduced the rest of Rick's family to Sandra and Philip. Her oldest friend from high school came with her husband, Aunt Dottie, her mother's sister, and all their friends from the ranch. They had a party full of their dearest friends and family. Everyone was having a fantastic time dancing to great music, drinking fine wine, and eating fabulous food.

She asked J.J. earlier to play one of Rick's favourites, "One Night at a Time," for their song. Looking in his direction, she nodded to let him know that it was time for them to take their dance. He winked back, letting her know that it would be the next one.

Turning to Rick, who was engaging in a conversation with Sean, she gracefully interrupted. "Excuse me, Sean, but I need to steal my husband for this next dance." Linking her arm through his, she led him to the dance floor. He smiled at her as he took her into his arms, and he spun her around the floor, dancing and enjoying himself immensely. They danced to their song and several others before each of his brothers stepped in to dance with the bride. He got his mother up on the dance floor along with his sister. He managed to dance a couple with Sandra and Sophie before they found each other again on the dance floor.

It was well after midnight when guests started to head out. They thanked everyone for joining them in their celebration of love and a new life together. J.J. had left over an hour ago, but they had their jukebox playing a variety of melodies as he took her for one last spin around the floor. They were the only ones left out in the garden.

"You make me the happiest woman alive. Thank you for everything, for taking the chance, for sticking through all of the rough spots, and for loving me," she said as she looked up into his eyes that were still partially covered by his Stetson and had just a hint of a gloss in them.

"Baby, you are the one that makes me so happy. I was just moving through life until I met you. In some strange way, I have your father to thank. It is unfortunate that it took his death to bring you home to me, but I will be forever in his debt." Placing his hand on her belly, he was about to continue when they both felt it. "Oh, my God, the baby just moved!" Astounded by the sensation, he looked down into her eyes. She was smiling.

"Yeah, I thought that it was happy nerves earlier when I felt it move. It felt like nervous butterflies…" She giggled, holding his hand longer on her belly.

Just then they heard a loud, wrenching scream from inside the house. Rick ran inside, and she was not far behind. They found Sandra at the bottom of the stairs clenching the bottom of her stomach and Philip not far behind coming down the stairs. She was still moaning, bent over on the floor.

"Oh, my God, Sandi…What's the matter, what can I do…" Amy was at her sister's side.

She looked up at her. "The hospital. It's time. The baby is coming…Phil…ip!" Another contraction overtook her, and all Amy could think was that it was too early for the baby to come. But she quickly got to the phone to advise the hospital that they were on their way. Philip dashed past her with her suitcase to get to the car. He quickly darted back inside to pick up his wife and carry her out to the waiting car.

"Do you need me to come to the hospital with you?" she asked her sister as she held her hand out to the car.

"Nooooo…" Another contraction interrupted. "Please stay here with Andrew. We will call when we know. Thanks. *Philip!*" She crunched his arm as he placed her into the car. They sped off.

Everyone in the house was awake now, except Andrew. She left him sleeping. Anna was downstairs, and Amy asked her to put on some coffee and herbal tea while they all sat and waited to hear the news. Curled up on the sofa, Rick left her while she napped. He figured that she needed her rest as well. He told his mom to go back to bed around two thirty, that he would stay awake and wait for the phone call. He thanked Anna for getting the coffee and tea and told them the same thing.

He sat in the big wing chair by the fireplace and thought about the first time that he saw Amy, and then he thought about the future and imagined them being at the hospital awaiting the delivery of their first child. Thinking about the pending arrival of their bundle of joy put a smile on his face. It was time to start thinking about names, he thought. He had no idea when the right time was to pick them out or anything about pregnant women, but it was about time that he learned. He still had a few more months to learn everything that he needed to learn. He wanted to understand what she was going through and how to make it easier for her. He made another mental note to read some of her maternity books.

He must have dozed off. He woke up to Andrew standing in front of him, tapping his arm and calling his name. "Uncle Rick…Uncle Rick, where's Mommy and Daddy?" his little, squeaky voice was asking.

He rubbed his face then lifted the boy into his lap. "Daddy had to take Mommy to the hospital last night. The baby was coming, and they needed the doctor." He spoke in the softest tone that he ever talked to anyone before in. He wasn't sure if he was saying the right things or not, but Andrew nodded as if he understood what he was telling him. He guessed that was a good thing. Amy watched from the doorway as he explained to Andrew what was happening. Just then the phone rang, and she quickly glanced at the clock—eight thirty in the morning. She picked up the phone. "Hello? Philip, good morning. How is Sandra?"

"Yes, everything here is fine. And Sandra?" Again she waited patiently for him to tell her that everything was all right. Finally, the answer that she was looking for. Her fears were gone.

"Everything went all right, the baby is doing fine and Sandra is resting. That it is good news. It's a boy."

"Congratulations. We will be there in a couple of hours. Okay, see you then. Give her a kiss for me. Love you both." She hung up the phone and walked over to Rick and Andrew.

Rick heard the one side of the conversation and understood that everything was fine. Amy bent down to explain it all to Andrew at his level. "Andy…Mommy and Daddy are okay. They are at the hospital with your new little brother."

"A brother, for me?" He jumped down from Rick's lap and ran toward the kitchen.

"I take it that he's good with that?" Rick asked, looking down at Amy as she took up residence on the floor in front of his feet with her arm resting on his lap, looking up at him.

"Yes, I do believe so."

They all had breakfast and went to the hospital to meet the newest member of their family, little Ivan Philip.

Everything in her life was in place, and it was the happiest that she had ever been.

Epilogue

It was their one-year anniversary, March 26. Rick was sitting in his office, going over the training schedule for Pride. That year they were taking her to the Kentucky Derby. Terry did them proud last year, true to his word. Pride won the Triple Crown, making her the first mare to win the Triple Crown in over three decades. It had been an awesome year. Three weeks after they took the Crown, their bundle of joy made her entrance into the world on September 29. She was perfect in every way. Weighing in at seven pounds and thirteen ounces, she twenty-three inches long, and with a head of beautiful blonde locks. Kassandra Patricia, Daddy's little foal. He was the proud poppa. Mystical Ranch once again had an Ivan and a Kassandra. Souls pass through the nights.

Susie announced that she was engaged and apologized that she would not be able to come back to work for them as she was staying in New York, which left the door wide open for his mother, who heard that they would not be having any help with the baby once they came home from the hospital. She came for a visit when Kasey was born and offered to stay for a spell to help out. Amy was thrilled with her offer. She enjoyed having his mother around.

The trial came and went. It turned out that they didn't need her testimony after all. Indigo was found not guilty, reason of self-defense and the fact that she was not the only person that he tried to blackmail. The tables got turned around and Jack was charged with blackmail and was currently serving his sentence in a county jail. Justice did prevail. Now she had the closure on that part of her life that she needed.

Fall arrived, and they were busy getting ready for the number of foals that were due in November. Their first one arrived on Remembrance Day. A fitting name was Sir Ivan. He was going to win them the Kentucky Derby someday, and they decided to keep their first one.

Amy was sitting in their family room nursing Kasey when she heard a knock at the door. From the kitchen, Alison called that she had the door, to not bother getting up. She heard Sophie's voice and called out to her, "Hey, Soph. I'm over here."

"Hey there, beautiful. How's Mommy doing today?" She cooed over Kasey, who looked up at her with one eye, still latched onto her breast.

"So what is up and brings you all the way out here that a phone call wouldn't do?" Amy asked her best friend.

"I have an offer for you. Before you say anything, just hear me out. You might be surprised…" She paused long enough to put down her bag and take a seat on the sofa across from Amy. "*Cosmo* wants you for the cover of their Mother's Day issue. You have a few days to ponder it over, but I think that it is a wonderful offer. You are still a hot commodity, you know. Everyone still wants to work with you. I will never understand your decision." She was talking as Amy was pondering the assignment. She did miss the work, the people. She was lost in her own thoughts as Sophie was still gabbing away about the assignment.

"All right, I will do it. But…" She broke off for a minute to switch sides as Kasey was getting agitated. "I want it done here, at our place. But before you confirm it with them, I need to discuss it with Rick first. It will be only one shot, Kasey and Mommy!" She shimmied in her seat to reach the edge to get up and put the baby into her bassinet to sleep and dress her top half.

Sophie was happily watching Amy and Kasey, her goddaughter, as she laid her down.

"I agree that it should be you and Kasey, but I was thinking more along the lines of an interview on how motherhood is treating you and how you are enjoying the family life," she chatted away. Amy was watching Kasey as she clutched her blanket and gurgled in her sleep when she heard Alison come into the room.

"Amy, I think that would be a great idea for you to do. Talk it over with Rick. I see how restless you are here," Alison said as she stood beside her and the baby.

"I don't think that Rick is going to object, but I will discuss it with him and let you know in a couple of days," she replied to both women as she turned away from the bassinet.

The three women chatted a bit longer over coffee and tea and then Sophie said it was time that she headed back to the city and she looked forward to Amy's call. She left her daughter in her grandmother's capable hands and walked her best friend to her car, giving her a kiss good-bye, and then she decided to go down to the stables and visit with Rick.

"Hey there, Bob…Have you seen the boss around?" She walked into the stables, glancing into the office, and didn't see him in there.

"Yeah…Over there in Sir Ivan's stall." He pointed to his left toward the stall.

She sauntered over, leaned over the railing, and saw him kneeling on the floor looking at the foal's hoofs. "Hey there, handsome…" she said, moving to the inside of the stall and plunking her butt down beside him.

Looking at her as he always did, adoringly, Rick responded with, "Come here. Give Daddy a kiss." He leaned over to reach her waiting lips. He had forgotten to come up for lunch, and it was late afternoon now. He was taking his wife out for a romantic dinner for their one-year anniversary. He put the horse's hoof down, took her by the arms to lift them both up, and walked her over to his office for some privacy. He hadn't had her in his arms for over ten hours. She was up before him this morning to feed Kasey. He closed the blinds and locked the door.

"Now come give me a proper kiss hello." He pulled her tight into his arms, placing his anxiously waiting lips against her hot, moist mouth. She tasted of raspberry tea. His tongue impatiently probed her lips apart and danced inside her mouth.

They came up for air. She pinned him up against the door and said, "I have a surprise for you." She kissed his cheek and then down his neck to whisper into his ear, "We are pregnant."

She took a step back, releasing him from her hold, looking into his expression. He was pleased. He had a grin from ear to ear. He lifted her up off her feet and swung her around the office, loudly pronouncing his excitement. "Yippeee…Yippee…Baby! You have made me the happiest man alive."

His life was just where he wanted it to be. He had the woman of his dreams, a family that he adored, and a very successful thoroughbred-breeding racing ranch. Life could not get any better.

THE END

WWW.BOOKSTRAND.COM/CHARLENE-PENFOLD

ABOUT THE AUTHOR

I was born in the late 60s. I am the eldest of two girls who have wonderful, loving parents. Our parents bought their dream home on a small lake in the country in Southern Ontario, where my sister and I grew up. A country girl at heart, I don't mind the hustle and bustle of the city either—for a visit.

I wrote my first book as a teenager under the guidance of my grade 10 English teacher, to whom I am grateful for his constructive criticism and help. I currently reside on a 300 acre farm in rural Southern Ontario with the love of my life and our two dogs, Coffee and Sasha, along with our cat Jasmine. *Souls Pass* is my first book published. I am looking forward to many more in the future. Even though *Souls Pass* was a long time in the making, I enjoyed every aspect of watching my characters come to life on paper. Although writing is my passion, I currently work at a local high school in the office. We enjoy quiet nights at home watching TV, especially NASCAR in season, with our furry family, and long walks or rides out on the farm.

Siren Publishing, Inc.
www.SirenPublishing.com

CPSIA information can be obtained at www.ICGtesting.com
Printed in the USA
LVOW130629130712

289856LV00004B/12/P

9 781622 411757